THE
GRAND
CHANGE

William Andrews

AC⊖RNPRESS

P.O. Box 22024
Charlottetown, Prince Edward Island
C1A 9J2
acornpresscanada.com

Printed in Canada by Marquis
Cover and interior design by Matt Reid
Cover photograph by John Sylvester

Library and Archives Canada Cataloguing in Publication

Andrews, William (William John Lloyd), author
The grand change / William Andrews.

Issued in print and electronic formats.
ISBN 978-1-927502-10-5 (pbk.).--ISBN 978-1-927502-14-3 (ebook)

I. Title.

PS8601.N4547G73 2013   C813.6   C2013-904713-1
                                              C2013-904714-X

Canada Council   Conseil des Arts
for the Arts   du Canada

The publisher acknowledges the support of the Government of Canada through the Canada Book Fund of the Department of Canadian Heritage and the Canada Council for the Arts Block Grant Program.

THE GRAND CHANGE

William Andrews

The Acorn Press
Charlottetown
2013

Masters of Their Own Realm

They had a simple philosophy: a penny-saved-penny-earned, don't-put-your-eggs-in-one-basket philosophy; a philosophy based on innovation, self-sufficiency, self-reliance and the art of making do. And not a book-learned philosophy but one relayed through past generations by those schooled in the art of survival.

Their mornings began with the crow of a rooster, or the whirr of an angry alarm clock, depending on the sun. When sundown came, the end of the usual day, they counted what little leisure there was as something to be treasured.

If they prayed, and some of them did, it was for a fighting chance. Nine times out of ten that was all they got; nine times out of ten that was all they needed. For their hands were deft and strong, they were confident in their own self-reliance and they took their satisfaction from the daily battles. They were masters of their own realm.

Prelude to Hook Road

For decades leading up to the nineteen-fifties, the people of Hook Road had seen little change. The last loads of mussel mud had been hauled and the more easily managed lime, obtained at railheads, was spread by machine rather than by shovel. Stumpers were no longer used, the days of major land clearing past. Horses no longer trod the revolving floors of horsepowers; the gasoline engine had been integrated. There were smaller changes: modifications in machinery, cold storage, radio, telephone. But other than that they in their little one hundred or so acre mixed farms knew life much the same as it was at the turn of the twentieth century.

Their farms were geared for self-sufficiency and to keep overhead down. Their land was strategically fenced for crop rotation; the stock nourished the land with its waste. The diversity of produce ensured a backup system; if they didn't make good on potatoes, there was pork, or beef.

They had orchards. They killed their own meat, churned their own butter, grew their own vegetables, raised their own poultry and collected their own eggs. They preserved food in cans, bottles, barrels of brine, cellars and cold outbuildings.

When it came to actual farming and transportation, they had the surest, most independent means of getting the job done. Their implements were simple, durable, easily repaired in a pinch—often with haywire and binder twine or the most basic of tools. These went hand in hand with manual labour and the horse, that most amazing, courageous, obedient beast, which, against mud, snow, cold, heat and drudgery, was virtually unstoppable.

The horse was the cog everything revolved around, even with its limitations, which pertained mainly to lack of speed.

Outside of the Saturday night trip to town, a train trip to the city during Old Home Week or a day of shopping maybe once a year, Hook Road people were Hook Road bound. This brought on a reliance among community members. Ensuing necessity brought out those who could double as midwives, veterinarians, blacksmiths, carpenters, fiddlers for the tymes. Hook Road had its own homegrown characters and comedians. Its hockey heroes learned their basic tricks on the nearest frog pond. And this all made for a tight-knit community where a man could rely on his neighbour for anything from a visit to an axe handle.

But change was in the making, had been for a number of years. Progress, stunted by a depression, was beginning to find its feet due to better economic times brought on by the Second World War. Compact tractors, adaptable to horse machinery, with pulleys to replace stationary engines, were available now and affordable through modern financing. Wider roads were being built, augmented by better graders, and snowplows kept them open for year-round motor travel. Electricity, which to this point had hummed its wires on main roads only, stood ready to move in with its ensuing conveniences.

These changes were not without allies: the effort of walking behind a gang plow from dawn to dusk, the dexterity, endurance and patience it took to tend the implement while keeping three horses in line and the constant chore of keeping the horses watered, fed, harnessed and hitched made it easy to acknowledge that a tractor would save much work. A moonlight ride in a pung sleigh with the fresh, chill air curling your breath may have held a certain romance, but when the cold ground drift swirled and cuffed, lashing white chill at your face, and the horse—at times barely visible—began bucking and plunging, it wasn't difficult to dream about the warmth and convenience of a car. Pumping water with a hand pump, washing clothes by hand and going to an outhouse in the middle of a snowstorm were excellent promotions for electricity.

There were other allies, of course, including TV and rock and roll, and they all conjoined and converged on Hook Road like a flood, with the anaesthesia that comes with easier, better times. Few questioned the outcome.

In actual fact, the sweep of change sounded the death knell to a way of life that had endured for over half a century. For Hook Road people, it was not unlike watching chaff being windblown from a barn floor with the barn doors open. And it was not so much the change, nor the loss, nor the gain the change wrought, but that something left, never to return.

Hook Road is fictional; the characters who live there are fictional, too. The rest, according to those who lived through such a time, including this writer, is based on historical fact.

Hook Road

CHAPTER 1

You can still recognize the road by its directions, dips and rises: the due north run from the Jar Road; that quick hump between the intersection and the crown of the short downgrade; the long, level slide; the sudden drop into the hollow; the slow rise to the hollow's north bank, where the road flattens briefly before sloping down to the creek; the low section to the swamp bog and beyond; the sudden hook west that gave the road its name; the final short jog to the front road that went about a mile northwest and spilled out into the village.

There are other reminders. The little brook in the hollow, spring fed from the low ground in a back field, still tinkles through the square, wooden tunnel with its creosote smell; the heavy, wooden bridge at the creek, often repaired and upgraded, is still a reasonable facsimile of what it once was;

the half-buried millstone still juts out from the creek's north bank as a remnant of the old mill; the swamp bog, in swamp tradition, still has its mangle of broken, awry, half-stunted trees.

But you won't find horseshoe picks or wagon-wheel ruts in the roadbed anymore. The bees don't hum along, touching down on blueberry bushes and wildflowers on the ditch banks. There is neither bush nor wildflower to be seen, only weeds and the odd scraggly tree. There are no cream-can stands or mailboxes at gateways; mostly there is not even a gateway to mark where they once stood. The houses, barns and outbuildings of the farmsteads are all gone; it's virtually impossible to random where they once stood. It's difficult to even random where the inner fencelines ran through the farm fields.

It's a wide, highly graded road now, well gravelled, its ditches deep and broad enough to hit brick clay, discouraging undergrowth and slough holes from runoffs. It was built to be used year-round, and it was, until a few years back when "closed" signs were put in from late fall through early spring. Access to croplands is its main purpose now.

But if you could go back to another time, a time when horses moved the scant implements and vehicles through fields of seeding and harvest. A time of dusty roads, foot-sucking mud and snow trails blurred by the white of winter. A time when liniment bottles, their necks poking through crowning cobwebs, cluttered the hand-hewn sills of horse stables, where jumbles of harness hung on steel hooks: oval collars with their pads, bridles with their blinders flopping sideways, curved hames poking here and there, drooping traces, hooped britchen and rope reins. A time when the walls of cow stables were decorated with manure-crusted stools, kicking chains, spray cans, shelved cans of DDT and tins of udder salve; when stookers with their stoop and squat formed the tent-like stooks to the thwacks of binders in the golden fields of fall and forkers forked the grain sheaves onto the veeing wagon racks where the builders built the load; when potato pickers bent in their trudge while whirligigs fanned out the tubers with their tails; when you could still hear the puck and hough of a stationary engine, the wrack-a-wrack-a-wrack of a thresher and the seethe haw of a crosscut saw in a winter-chilled woodlot, the bump of wood sleigh runners in the pitches, the creak of a hand pump. If you could go back to that time, you would know that what now is a by-road, an in-road, was an artery into part of a thriving community.

It was a sunken road then; two wagon rigs could pass but with not a lot of room. It was hard and dusty in the summer, more like a ditch in wet times and when the winter came it would sleep and be no more a road than the fields beside it, recognized only by the twin fencelines running on its banks.

It would slowly reappear with the sinking of the snows, familiar, but foreboding now—its banks grey-brown and spiking bare bushes, dead weeds, grasses and small trees; its bed worm-lined and gutted by runoffs; and with flat, deceptively smooth beds of muck at the sloughs.

Then, that which gave it purpose, the traffic of plodding horses and wagons, almost bucking through its mire, would appear.

It was quite an ordinary road, seeing little of the unusual

except for the odd pack peddler or a stranger looking for work, or his way. Those who travelled it went hand in hand with the dreams, hopes, defeats and scant victories it had known for all its time.

My great grandfather watched it turn from a pair of wheel ruts running between the farmsteads to a crude wagon path, saw it begin to sink with the gradual rise of its banks from runoff erosion and the scrape of horse-drawn, stone-loaded drags hauled sideways.

My grandfather walked it carrying a muzzle-loading shotgun to shoot the black ducks that would huddle in the millpond, when there was a millpond, and the mill supplied the area with grist. He walked it from the village train station, home from the Great War, his mind confused and his inner being shattered. He hauled home the last load of grist produced at the mill on it. He brought my grandmother home as his bride in a light wagon on it.

My father drove my mother home on it to start their married life together in the same light wagon.

He drove in the same wagon to the village church to bury my mother upon her death at my birth.

I often walked the road. I cursed it when I had to wade around slough holes but I loved it when my bare feet would scuff up dust in its summer-dry bed. It held a mystery then, with small birds twittering and flittering through the low trees and bushes at its banks and with bees busy at the flowers there. Usually, I would be heading to or from school. But sometimes I would be heading for the creek, perhaps in an evening with the others to gather at the bridge and do our harmless foolishness, our voices and laughter rising above the rush and splatter of the water falling from the spillway of the back-sprung old mill, with its awry shingles and bulging sides. Perhaps it would be on a Sunday, or on a seasonal farm break, with the brown fishing line wrapped on the broken end of the alder pole I used last time in my pocket and the old army knife with its square blade and punch tied to my belt with a string. Others would be at the bridge too and the bright excitement off a fish hole would mingle with the summer breeze on our faces and in our hair and with the pleasant sun on our shoulders. And we would cut the alder poles and wrap the line on the end, then drape over the bridge on our bellies, swinging the line under. There would be that hollow plunk of the sinker hitting the water, then the sudden tugs, then the *splunge* in the water and the wriggling fish arcing through the air with the upswing of the line to land smack on the bridge bed, to curl, dust-patched, with that stare.

But my favourite memory is of riding down the road in a truck wagon with my father, heading to the little town for goods. I was a very small boy then. It is the first thing in life I can remember.

I suppose it took over an hour to go the seven miles to town. The steel wagon wheels, thick-spoked and heavy-hubbed, clattering on the rough road; the long wagon box creaking its song, remnants of chaff, seed oats and potato sprouts jigging on its rough bed.

Our seat was a board placed crosswise on the box sides. I sat upright and alert, my feet dangling above the wagon bed. My father sat hunched over, his forearms, with folded shirt sleeves, resting on his thighs near the knee patches of his overalls, his large, calloused hands loosely holding the rope reins with their ends dangling and furling round his pant cuffs and worn boots. His eyes, peering through the shadow of his cap peak, had a tired, sleepy look.

The horse moved in a steady plod, his tail swishing lazily around the britchen wrapping his rump. Once in a while, his ears would do their dip and point—sometimes from the pass of an infrequent car, sometimes from the flip of the reins on his long, hollow back summoning a faster pace.

In time, the clatters and creaks began to soothe as the road turned to grey asphalt with tarred cracks running along square storefronts.

As we came into town, the warm, sultry wind lazily stirred the odd loose scrap of paper lying in the near vacant streets. A round sign, nestled in the arc of a steel pole by a gas pump, waved its shadow over the pump's disc head, glass cylinder tank and looping, hung hose; its creak added to the afternoon's dry humdrum as we passed by. The small shop-like garage beside the pump smelled heavily of gasoline, rubber and grease and had a square car out front with its engine's side covers folded up like a bat's wings.

The smells of crushed oats and various animal feeds came to us as we sided the ramp that fronted the feed mill warehouse. The attendant there had the same sleepy, tired look as my father. His voice sounded sleepy as well in their scant conversation. He threw down bloated bags of cow concentrate and pig starter that bounced slightly on the wagon bed, and handed down a receipt that my father stuffed into the bib of his overalls. From the hardware store, as we drove up and parked by its high windows, came the smells of oiled harnesses and hemp ropes. From my perch on the wagon seat, through the windows, I saw collars, pads and hames with their buckles and straps hanging on a wall. Below them, shovels, axes and forks reclined. To their left, a barrel stood with various tool handles protruding from its mouth and muskrat traps hanging from its lip.

I watched my father climb the store's worn wooden steps and walk through its doorway, his form growing faint in the darkened storeroom. When he emerged, he gingerly carried a ball of barbed wire. The stocky storekeeper, in an apron, followed with a plowshare in one hand and a fork handle in the other. The wire ball thumped, the plowshare clunked and the fork handle rattled as they were placed on the wagon bed.

The two men stood then for a while, talking of prices, the coming election and the best horse liniment. The breeze tousled the scant sprigs of hair horseshoeing the bald on the storekeeper's head as friendly so longs were exchanged and he made his way back into the store.

We pulled up to the small grocery store then and stopped beside the window case where there was a pasteboard sign of a Coke girl smiling with a wink. The doorbell tinkled its welcome as we went in, my father carrying two crock jars. I stood waiting and watching on the heaving board floor amidst the smells of stale oranges, smoked herring and cream soda pop. I could hear the tick-tock of the square clock on the wall above the hum of the water-filled pop cooler down at the far end of the long counter.

Through the open door to the storage room, I saw the store-keeper twist the spigot handles on reclining molasses and kerosene drums and squat, watching their contents pour into loop-handled, round-lipped measuring cans he used to fill the crock jars. Later, the storekeeper scooped beans from a barrel by the counter and shuffled them into a brown paper bag. Then, rocking a large knife, he cut a wedge out of the cheese disc and weighed it on the scales sitting squat near the disc on the counter. Brown paper crinkled and rustled as he swiped a sheet from the steel-framed roll sitting next to the cheese disc, wrapped the cheese and tied the package with a string running from a shelved spool through a hanging steel eye.

Then we took the groceries (there was a bag of rolled oats, a bag of sugar and a caddy of tea as well) to the wagon.

Cold storage wasn't far away and we walked there, leaving the horse, his sleepy head hanging and one foot resting, untied by the store.

The stick-handled door opened with a swirling fog of frost and we made our way down a narrow corridor with tiers of ice-encased lockers on either side, stopping at the one we had rented. My father opened it and a white puff surged out as he retrieved a roast of beef wrapped in brown paper. As he closed the locker, I couldn't help thinking of some iced-up castle I saw in some fairy tale book.

The coldness of the place made the heat of the afternoon outside seem strange. My father watched my feeble attempt to climb up on a wagon wheel before boosting my behind with his hand. Then he walked stiffly across the street to a small shop with a large steel Players sign nailed to its side.

He returned with two small ice cream cones and handed one to me as he climbed onto the wagon. We sat then, quietly biting at the ice cream for a while.

The horse, in his sleepy pose, was still except for the odd tail swish at a bothersome fly. A piece of paper scuttled by, swept by the breeze, its scuffle mingling with the creak of the sign still waving its shadow not far away.

The sleepy, tired look seemed to deepen in my father's eyes as he took the reins in his free hand and, reining the horse, wheeled the wagon in mid street. The inside wheel scraped against the wagon box with a protesting screech. Once more the clop of the horse's feet resounded in the quiet streets and, as peacefully and unnoticed as we clattered into town, we clattered out.

I don't recall too much about Hook Road on our way to town—too excited, I guess. But on the way home I remember how different things looked from the opposite side, something that has reminded me ever since of two sides of life.

The trip we all took to see my father off to war I can recall as being filled with confusion and fear.

We drove down the road without conversation on a clear, early summer day. A strange foreboding rode with us, and it carried into the old station house where we sat on pew-like benches in the waiting room with its pot-bellied stove. The smells of old varnish, coal dust and stale tobacco spit seemed to add to the dry, vacant atmosphere and the foreboding. From the office, behind the high ticket window, the rattle of the Morse code receiver echoed loud and hollow like all the other sounds, be they squeak, scrape or bump.

Then there was a faint vibration. The crossing bell sounded from the roadway by the potato warehouse, its clang muted by the station walls. The hands of ticket holders began checking belted suitcases and paper shopping bags. The vibration increased rapidly. You could hear it now. Soon it was a rumble. The panes in the high windows began to ping. An old man on one of the ledge-like benches, fixed in the grooved walls, spit a stream of tobacco juice into a cuspidor beside him.

The rumble became deafening and seemed to have lift as we made our way out to the board platform, stepping around an attendant manoeuvring a high-backed, high-wheeled baggage wagon by its D-handled tongue.

I had a feeling of excitement mingled with awe and dizziness as I watched the big black engine, weaving ever so slightly with the rails, *pumpf, pumpf, pumpf* its way past. With the crank of its drivers and the turn of its wheels, half hidden by steam curls and with grey-black smoke billowing from the short stack next to the clanging bell on its long black snout, it was as if it was bursting from a cloud. I wondered how something so huge and powerful could be controlled by the man with the high, striped cap in the square cab window, but his look was unconcerned.

Soon the rumble and vibration began to fade into innocent creaks. The steam curls trailed off. The clacks of the coupling joints spaced out. The weave of a passing coach grew lazy. Suddenly it all came to a screeching shunt with domino clunks of ramming car couplings and a blast of steam.

I can't remember exactly what my father said when he squatted to shake my hand and say goodbye; I can only remember the sadness that seemed to hang like a veil in his eyes and on his face.

The trip with my grandfather to school for my first day was less fearful, but not by much. It was a gloomy September day to start with, almost at the point of rain. There was no conversation that time either. When we pulled up to the school, standing in its own gloominess, its paint-worn shingles and waterspouts adding to its grim demeanour, I sat frozen to the wagon seat, looking up the worn stone steps leading to the porch door, with most of its brown paint worn off and its doorknob hanging awry. My grandfather cleared his throat, his hands fumbling with the reins. Presently, he rolled up his hip and reached into his pocket for a brown-cornered nickel and handed it to me. His voice was frank and quiet when he spoke. "Go ahead, Jake," he said. "You'll be all right."

I climbed down from the wagon and stood watching my grandfather drive away, hearing the hoof clops and wheel clatters fade into the distance, feeling totally alone. Slowly, I climbed the steps and entered the porch, which was cool and smelled of dustbane and pine oil. The door to the classroom needed only a push; the knob and lock were completely gone from the hole, which was jagged and knife-cut. The door opened with a creak that echoed loudly in the empty, high-ceilinged room with its large south windows. To this day, I can still see the step-flattened bubble gum patches cemented to the floor and the initial-scarred desks sitting on their rails with their curved seats flipped up. They seemed to herd past the pot-bellied stove and jam toward the broad desk standing before the blackboard. And I stood in the dry, wondering atmosphere of the first day waiting for what was to come. It was a long wait, for a long day. My trip home that day gave little relief because I knew I would have to return the next day.

Then there was the longest trip home. The day the telegram came. It was a crisp, clear autumn day without even a whisper of a breeze. It's a day I not only remember pretty much in its entirety, but I can still feel.

Wally Mason and I walked to the village early that morning. We had a few cents from collecting beer bottles and decided to buy some licorice pipes from the canteen behind the station, where old Sam Dougan sold cigarettes, candy and pop and kept a pinball machine and a punch board.

We stood on the station platform munching on the licorice, waiting for the school bell to ring. Farther down the track, the men at the potato warehouse were loading a boxcar with hand carts, walking straight-backed and rigid for balance, bobbing their way over the heaving ramp between the warehouse landing and the boxcar, the ears of the potato bags flopping like pigs' ears.

Suddenly, the *putt, putt* of a trolley coming into the village broke in. We watched it pull up to the station, seething out billows of blue smoke. Two section hands, seated low in its seats, peered coon-like around its square shield. The men, in their greasy striped overalls and high caps, rose from their perches and, teetering the machine on its toy-like wheels, moved it off the rails to the side of the station platform. Then, taking their long, steel lunch cans and a point-headed mallet apiece, they walked past the platform. "Nice day, fellows," one of them said. We agreed. The bell clanged for school, the noise somewhat muted by the distance. As we started off, I heard the men talking in casual tones.

"Think the war will soon be over, Bill?"

"Yeah. They're getting things pretty well under control."

It was a usual day at the schoolhouse with those echoing sounds: the hoarse, urgent whispers; the spit balls dinging the ears; the angry strap and the fearful *awooo!*; the scribbling bustle; the mispronounced words of the reader; the hesitant, try-again attempts of the speller, standing bug-eyed with mouth agape in the spelling line. Then the knock came, abrupt and singular.

I watched the teacher move from her desk and open the door. I looked over her shoulder and noticed the sprig of hair wisping from her bun into the wedge of clear between the partly open door and the jamb. Slowly, my grandfather's face appeared, swathed in a greyness that matched his capless head. There was a stark defeat in his eyes and his mouth was drawn tight. When the teacher turned, she had the same grave greyness about her face and her eyes were big and when they turned to me they had a bewildered stare. Things hung for a while before she turned back to The Old Man and I saw her shoulders stiffen. She closed the door and paused with her back to the class, then turned as if in some kind of trance and slowly made her way to me. She took a deep breath, let it out and opened her mouth to speak, but it froze open and her eyes fluttered and grew misty and pained. She squared off her shoulders and swallowed hard. "Your grandfather has come for you, Jake," she said, her voice almost a whisper. "He wants you to go home with him." She moved to her desk and stood watching me with the pain growing in her eyes.

Everybody sat watching, grey and frozen, while I fumbled with my books until I got them into the old army pack I used as a school bag. "Everybody back to work," the teacher said, her voice too soft to have much command.

It seemed like a year went by before I got to the door. My grandfather sat hunched over in the wagon, looking small and withered. The greyness seemed to hang on him like flour on a mill hand. He had his cap peak low. I could barely see his eyes.

He did not watch me climb the round, steel mount step on the wagon box and sit beside him. He flipped the reins and, saying nothing, drove to the village and pulled up at the canteen. He sat rigid for a while before handing me a dime, his movements stiff and pondering. "Get a chocolate bar, Jake," he said, his voice harsh and strange.

I never like to think about the trip home, the coloured leaves on the trees and bushes on the roadbanks and what green there was left in the grass, all veiled by stiff, cold greyness. It's hard enough to think about my grandfather unhitching the horse with the grey defeat hanging on him, and him staying in the barn while my grandmother stood in the door, her eyes reddened and her face flushed and puffy. Or about her sitting beside me on my bed, hugging me close, her sobs and heavy sighs spacing between the words that wouldn't sentence until they came out with stark finality: "Dear, Waldron's been killed in the war." The minister at the pulpit speaking in morbid tones; the veterans parading and saluting with stiff, grave, faces; the lonely, haunting bugle calls; Mabel Mason sitting with my grandmother, patting her hands and comforting her; they're all are difficult to think on, but the trip home the day the telegram came is next to impossible.

My grandparents took me from there. I called her Nanny. I called him Gramps when he was around, The Old Man or The Boss when he wasn't. Not out of disrespect; it was common in those days. We had the first farm on the south end of Hook on the western side. Its most distinguishing feature was that the farm buildings centred the farm near the western boundary with a lane running to Hook and another to Jar, which ran along our southern boundary. We were known as the Jacksons: Harvey, Ella and me, Jake.

Prelude to Autumn on Hook Road

"Once the exhibition is over, the fall is here," went the saying along Hook Road, and around August twenty-second the chill crept into the air and those crisp, clear days came. Soon the farmers began hauling out their binders, those senseless-looking humps of angles, cogs, rollers, canvas and rods, each with a cutting bar, a lever poking here and there and something resembling a riverboat paddlewheel. And they took flat sticks and packed that heavy black grease into grease cups among the works, on the side wheels and on that big, cleated wheel underneath at the centre of gravity, which bore nearly everything and everything ran off. And they inspected the canvas belt that rolled on its floor and the two smaller ones that rolled counter-wise and upright, then patched the tears and fray holes from last year's work. And they gnashed the triangular cutting bar teeth against hand-cranked grindstones, grinding them into shape. On the next trip to town, they bought the cross-wound twine balls in tarpaper with an end sprigging from the centre hole.

As the days grew steadily cooler and the yellow transparent apples began to ripen and the grain was rapidly turning from a green-yellow patchwork to gold, they walked through their stands amidst the pungent smells of mustard weed and floating thistledown. And they rubbed the grain kernels between their palms and looked at the sky, their minds mulling on when to start the harvest. With potato digging in close proximity, timing was crucial and the weather, always the weather. They consulted their almanacs. Some held to animal habits: dogs eating grass, bee behaviour, chicken antics. Some pondered on the moon. Some just went by chance like everybody else. Nothing was constant or totally predictable, except that there would be long, drawn-out drudgery ahead. And they steeled themselves as for a marathon.

On his chosen day, a farmer fed his horses oats against the coming trudge and buckled on the messes of harness and hitched them to the binder's double tree. The horses would be gimpy from pasture freedom since haying, but with terse commands and rein slaps they would run the binder into the field for the first pass.

Then there was action in every corner, with the driver bouncing on the tail-like seat, one foot strapped to the sheaf carriage trip. With an eye to the horses, the rolling canvas, the paddlewheel sweeping grain into the cutting bar, the twine running through an eye here and there from the ball can to the knotter, the filling sheaf carriage for the trip at the windrow. And it didn't hurt to look behind once in a while for loose sheaves or a cog or something that decided to take off on its own. With a hand to a lever to adjust for rough ground in rein juggle and an ear for alien sounds from the cutting bar, the packer, the kicker, the grain rushing through the works. If there was room left he could think about dinner. And there likely be would be stops, curses, kicks, skinned knuckles and a trench through the stubble from a jammed centre wheel.

Eventually, the bugs would get worked out, the various components and actions would harmonize, the horses would fall into their rhythm, pulling as one. Around the field they went to the stutter of the cutting bar and the thwack of the kicker kicking out sheaves. Gradually, the ragged windrows would begin to lengthen.

Looking insignificant in the theatres of the fields, with the constant rustle of the sheaves and the stubble underfoot, tucking sheaves under their arms, bending with a slight squat to set them head to head to form the stooks, the stookers worked, pausing now and then to bind a loose sheaf with a hand-knotted band of grain stalks. Their arms and chests chafed from the thistles and nettles packed in the sheaves. And if it was early morning, a dew would give strength to the chafing and their arms, pant legs and shirt fronts would be soaked. In time, the fields lay like golden brushes, spotted densely with the stooks, standing by their short shadows like so many miniature tents.

Then, with spiked-together racks flanging at the sides, the cross-boarded uprights awry, the wagon rigs in their lazy rock moved in and the forkers heaved on their forks, arm working against arm, sweeping the stook sections high and onto the load, where the builders built, placing the sheaves around the racks' square perimeter, sometimes flipping them to get the butts out.

Some days, a bright, golden stillness filled the fields, disturbed only by the hums of hummingbirds, the rustles of sheaves, the tinkles of trace links, the rattles of harnesses as horses shook their noses at nose flies. But the cold winds came, too, growing increasingly bitter, and the forkers fought gusts of wind that could sweep fork loads away. Sometimes, after an overly heavy rain, they had to tear down the stooks and spread them to dry. But they rolled steadily on until the horse hooves clopped on the barn floors for the last trip and the last sheaves were forked in relay up walls of sheaf butts in the lofts.

Then, as in the changing acts of a play, the scenes along Hook Road changed. Whirligig potato diggers, their rear ends fanning like tails of peacocks, sweeping clay and potatoes against their canvas booms, crept along potato drills while the digger men hunched on stemming seats like sleepy crows, guiding the sets of pole-divided horses in a relentless plod.

Spaced the lengths of the fields, bobbing like multicoloured clothespins on lines, hoisting their baskets in underbelly swing, clawing like digging dogs to clear away the tops and flip the potatoes into the baskets, the pickers hunched and trudged. At their sides, filling bags stood in their ragged rows like dummies, their loose mouths flopping in the breeze like unruly mops of hair. Here and there along the lines, pickers rose and stepped out to squat, thigh-set their basket, bag-mouth its rim and dump. Along the ragged rows, the low-slung sloven rigs with their high back wheels moved, while the loaders, with a knee boost, hoisted the filled bags by their mouth corners.

When daylight began to fade, the diggings were harrowed over and the pickers gleaned, moving and picking like pecking robins. Finally they came home from the fields, their clay-caked boot heels clopping on wheel paths, their strides stiff but gratefully free from the back-bent trudge, the lingering clay choke still in their nostrils, its grit still in their eyes and fingernails.

From the sides of houses, at the foundations, came the cobbles of the day's last potatoes being rolled down cellar holes, and the drivers with their sloven rigs moved faint in gloom as they faded away for the day. From kitchen windows, kerosene lamps shed their mellow comfort, their extending basks spreading like hope across footpaths shadowed by duckweed. In kitchens came the rattles of dishes and murmurs of voices at the plots of suppers. In gloomy porches, somewhat subdued now, the workers filed, taking their hand-washing turns at sink pumps with a flub of yellow lye soap and a hand wipe on an endless towel on rollers; their mind-stomach coordinations fixed on the heavy farm fare of meat, potatoes, thick gravy and bread puddings steaming on parlour tables.

Autumn on Hook Road

CHAPTER 2

There is always a point when seeds of change begin to take root. That point, which was to bring irreversible change to Hook Road, came on a clear autumn morning. The sun had risen singular in a cloudless sky to beam down hotly, glistening the melted frost on the browning weeds and grass on the banks of the headland. There was no wind. The caw of a crow rang clear and trumpet-like from the maple woods shadowing the south edge of our potato field.

I was working east on the last dug potato row, feeling lank, thinking about dinner, when I heard The Old Man mutter, "Must be thinking about another election." I paused in my hunch, rested my hands on the basket handle and looked up.

The Old Man stood looking across the potato field, barren except for the odd scraggly top sprigging here and there and two full rows with their tops lying like matted hair at the field's south fringe. His empty, woven basket sat squat and awry by the half-filled bran bag he had dumped it into. His canvas gloves, clay-caked at the palms, lay draped over the basket's carved wooden handle.

I straightened and followed the direction of his gaze to the intersection of Jar and Hook. A red half-ton truck with black lettering was parked there, and on Jar's bank a man was knee-deep in bushes sighting down Hook through a theodolite. Along the spaced posts of the fenceline a couple of hundred yards down, another man stood with a pole.

The Old Man dropped his gaze to the plug of tobacco in his left hand and the open jackknife in his right. Absently, he carved off a chew, slid it off the blade into his mouth and, in double motion, clasped the knife, stowed it with the tobacco into his pants pocket and began slowly working his cud, his eyes sweeping back across the field.

Nanny finished filling her basket with a handful of potatoes, rose, thigh-set her basket, limp-footed her way to the bran bag and dumped, the cobbling sound of the potatoes breaking the near-total silence. She hedge-stepped then to beside The Boss, her eyes watching with his.

Standing in their ragged coats and overalls, caked with clay at the knee patches, they made an odd pair. The Old Man was bean-pole thin, his shoulder stoop augmenting his overly long nose, deep-set eyes and flat cheeks falling to a square jaw. Nanny was short and stout, her grey-brown hair sweeping back from a moon face into her rooster-tail bandana, her old grey winter coat flaring in straight fall from the one button at the neck to the red band of her rubber boots.

an spat out tobacco and reached for his gloves.
.r without trouble this afternoon," he said, work-
.s gloves over his large hands. "I guess we'll load up for dinner when we finish this row."

He swiped up his basket and moved to fall on his knees at the wide scatter of potatoes, some nubbing half-hidden in the clay beside hooped-down tops. Nanny followed suit and the two with their knee waddle, hoisting their baskets forward, picking like pecking crows, began closing in on me.

The day had begun as a usual potato harvest day, with a sleepy, foot-chilling grope down the stairs and into the kitchen, where the cold made the smells of kerosene and setting bread dough almost morbid. The scratch, snap and sulphur whiff of the match at the table lamp, the flair of flame in the wick slot, the sudden bask of light with the fitted globe revealing Nanny's sleep-drawn face and dishevelled hair seemed to crack off the day.

Nanny stuffed yesterday's paper into the stove with kindling and lit the fire while The Boss and I worked on our clay-stiffened coarse boots at the couch and got our coats and caps from their wall hooks, our shadows bobbing and weaving on the wall like pointing spooks. The Old Man lit the lantern hanging on a nail in the porch and clunked down the wired-in globe. I swiped milk buckets from their nails and we went out of the porch and across the yard. A bask of light, pushed by foot shadows, waggled around The Boss's feet, its reflection revealing at times the light-blanked eyes of the seven milk cows waiting in the yard.

The Boss paused by the cow stable door, allowing me to

identify it, then moved a few yards farther up to the little door leading into the barn floor, where the morning hump of hay lay. I threw back the stable door and the cattle filed in and found their stalls. I hung the buckets on the wall by feel and groped beside the cows, linking their tie chains. A thin shaft of light cutting along a lap gap gave a quick direction and I got a stool and a bucket and got squatted beside the first cow, clasping the bucket between my knees.

A stream of urine hissed in the darkness, its smell mingling with the tangy stink of manure. I could hear the cow's belly sounds with my head against her flank, and it was all warm and comforting. As I fumbled for her teats, I found it hard to stay awake. The *ping-squish* of the milk hitting the pail brought bleats from the chorus of cats badgering for milk. From the next stable came the thump of horse hooves and the odd soft nutter. Neck chains rattled as The Old Man flopped open the laps in the barn floor wall. Rectangles of light showed at the heads of the cows and there was the swish of hay-supplement for a waning pasture and munches in the mangers.

Milking didn't take long; the cows had next year's calves growing in their bellies and except for the farr cow, we were weaning them dry. The crooked-backed cream separator in the porch, with its large bowl, bucket seats, spouts and crank gave its angry whirr only briefly; only a small *blurp* of cream for the can cooling in the cellar hole, barely a token of skim milk for the calf tub in the small pasture by the house.

It was warm by then, in the kitchen. The cold, morbid smells had been driven out by the hot stove, its lights dancing out cheer through its several cracks. Instead, there were the toasty smells of burning maple, cooked oatmeal and tea. The snap and burr of the fire wove their way through the *whoot* of the kettle boiling out steam and the strains of an old-time fiddle and guitar twang from the radio. There was pause after breakfast, for The Old Man to lean back in his chair and smoke his pregnant cigarette and catch the news and weather. After Nanny washed the dishes, in a large pan on the stove, she kneaded dough on the table, stuffed knife-cut globs into pans, slid them into the oven, filled the stove with wood and set the draft.

First light was beginning to creep in by the time we got the horses hitched to the sloven and picked up Nanny at the pathway to the house. The rattle of the sloven wheels, the foot clumps of the horses and the tinkles of trace chains resounded eerily as we rode to the field. I moved to the pile of empty bags at the back of the sloven before we turned in at the headland. The cold, choky dust from the bags puffed into my face as I threw them at intervals while we drove the length of the field by the potato drills. When we hitched the horses to the digger, you could begin to see the tops on the rows. When The Boss swung the horses into the outside row, their feet muddling in cross-step, you could see small steam puffs coming from their nostrils. After, The Boss halted the horses at the row's end, waited for me to lever down the digger's shear, then drove on. You could see the side whirl of the clawing digger's wheel and the spew of clay and potatoes hitting the side-slung canvas boom with a *carrumph*.

It was close to midday when we finished the row. The red truck had not moved, but the two men had set up down the road a ways. Nanny lumbered to the house to start dinner. The Old Man and I turned to the horses, which stood hitched to the digger, lazily swishing their tails, and changed them to the sloven. We ran along the row of filled bags then, the horses stopping on command, The Old Man knee-boosting the bags onto the sloven, me taking and dragging them to some kind of pile against the axle box.

At the headland by the road, loaded now, we drove to the corner of the field by the end of the lane and stopped. I jumped off and went for the mail. As I was returning, the red truck passed; the sun glinted on the driver's glasses and deepened his partner in shade. The driver gave a formal wave. The Old Man waved back and we were engulfed in the dust trail of the truck. The Old Man winced his shoulder at the dust and turned the horses toward home.

There was a pensive look on his face I had rarely seen before as we rode down the lane, the wheel jolts flapping the mouths of the bags we sat among, sending minute puffs of choky dust into our faces. When he pulled up beside the house, he over-shot the cellar hole and had trouble getting backed around and wound up taking a turn around the house to get lined up. When he began letting the filled bags down the cellar hole to me, his hands worked in a ponder. More than once, he absently let down a bag open-end first, sending a barrage of loose potatoes and dust at me, augmenting my agony of having to crawl, haul dumping on my belly, to the corner where the potatoes were piled to within a few feet of the floor joists. Different times, as we unhitched the horses and watered them, lead them to their stalls and their dinner, his head shot toward the road.

After a dinner of potatoes, thick slabs of pork, jimmies and thick gravy, topped off with bread pudding with raisins, we sat in the drowsy warmth of the kitchen, with the sun slanting through the window and cutting through the wave of tobacco smoke hovering above The Old Man. He was sitting sprawled sideways across the couch, hidden from the waist up by the newspaper he was reading. The farm noon radio was running the deaths, stock prices and news. Nanny, with the dishes done, had somehow found the incentive to knit. I sat flopped in the armchair by the radio, one foot resting on the steel end of the couch, in some kind of drowse, the whine of the dying kettle, the clicks of Nanny's knitting needles and the drone of the radio drifting at me as in a dream.

Different times during the news The Old Man, listening while he read, called to Nanny for a prompt, something he only did when his mind was distracted by something.

The tiredness grabbed me then, boxing me in, and it was hard to break out when The Old Man's feet thumped the floor. We had the horses out of their stalls and half hitched before I fully snapped to life.

We finished in mid-afternoon. As we worked, The Old Man looked intermittently toward the road, and when we rode from the field, desert-like now with the skeletal digger standing singular and lonely, he glanced once more.

John Cobly came that evening at about the time when the weariness of the day had given way to relaxation and it was good to read the funny papers with my feet on the stove's oven door. Nanny was clicking her needles close to the lamp side of the table. The Old Man sat hunched at the end, musing at solitaire, working his dog-eared cards in shadowy flops. The clicks, flops, burr of the fire and hum of the kettle were spacing into a comedy show on the radio with its patented laughs.

John was a stubby little man with a pinkish face and freckles. Most called him "bran face" when he wasn't around. His farm was just west of the swamp bog on the west side of the road. There was just him and his wife, Agnes, working their farm with seasonal help. Their daughter was married to a banker in the city. Their two sons were in the Air Force.

He came twirling in around the door without waiting for an answer to his knock and flopped into the armchair. Nanny and I returned his greeting. The Old Man just grunted without a pause in his solitaire.

John paused for a few moments in the armchair, then rose and stood over The Boss, peering down his nose, his eyes shifting with the card flops. "King of diamonds on the queen, Harv... You missed the ten," he said, his words bursting almost in sync with the punchlines of the radio comedy. "You missed the six of clubs; you're never going to win that way, Harv. But maybe that's your strategy?" The Old Man just kept flopping the cards in his muse.

John Cobly settled back down in the armchair. "What are you knitting, Ella?" he said. Nanny held up a half mitt with the needles angling from a decapitated-like thumb. John shook his head.

"Don't know how you do that. With my ten thumbs there would be needles sticking out of me all angles. I'd look like a pincushion."

"How's Agnes these days?" Nanny said.

"Cranky as ever… Ah, she's all right. Burnt up a cake this afternoon, covered it up with an inch of frosting—all the better. But she can't be too bad off. Puts up with me and the Cape Britoners we got hired for the digging."

John Cobly took an open pack of tobacco from the bib of his overalls, slid out the paper pack stuck in the cellophane wrapping, leafed out a paper, pinched tobacco from the pack, spread it on the paper trough and began twisting a cigarette. He peered up at me, his fingers and thumbs working, his eyes glinting from the shadow of his cap peak.

"Into some heavy reading are you, Jake?"

"Heavy enough for me," I said. Another burst of laughter came from the radio. John Cobly smirked at a punchline, then ran his tongue across the paper edge and twisted up the roll.

The Old Man finally lost his game. He packed up the cards and put them in his corner shelf at the head of the couch by the flue box. Then he swiped his makings from the window ledge, slumped down sideways across the couch and began rolling a cigarette.

"Turn the radio off, John," The Old Man said.

"Sure you don't want to finish it, Harv?" John said. "Sometimes you can get a laugh out of them."

"Sometimes you can and sometimes you can't; hear them too much and it all starts to sound the same."

John Cobly turned off the radio and sat with his cigarette dangling unlit in his mouth, a match in his fist, his thumb on the head, waiting for The Old Man to finish. Then the snap of the match flaring into light broke into the quiet from the absence of radio sounds. John reached to light The Old Man's cigarette, lit his own, moved to the stove, poked the spent match through a draft hole and went back to the armchair.

"I suppose you mind when the radios first came, Harv?" John Cobly said.

"Yeah, Uncle Joe had one in town, earphones and a battery big enough to fill a wheelbarrow."

"Television will be the next thing, Harv."

The Boss settled back, blowing out a belch of smoke. "Think there's much to them?"

"Kind of like watching a picture show in a box. Fred James got one. Seen it one evening when I was settling up. Lot of snow. I wasn't too crazy about it. They say they're catching on, though."

"More tomfoolery than anything else, probably," The Old Man said. There was a pause. A sudden gust of wind creaked the old house.

"Got your crop in, Harv?"

"Yeah, got it in; been a pretty good fall. All I got don't amount to much anyhow."

"Sometimes I think we'd all be better off keeping it small like you, Harv. Potatoes are such a gamble."

"How are you getting along?"

"Not bad. The Cape Britoners I got had a bit of a set-to the other night—got into the hooch, hammered each other around the yard for a while. Had to send a couple home. But that's the way she goes. We're getting there. Sometimes you wonder if you should be at something else, but it's a living I guess."

John Cobly leaned back in the armchair, shot his legs straight out and folded his arms across his belly. His cigarette dangled askew from his lips. "Thought I'd like to be a doctor when I was a gaffer. But by the time I learned to even read and write, with all the time off for cropping and whatnot, I had trouble fitting into the seats. I mind watching the others going to school and me just getting in with a load of mud."

"You would have made a good doctor, John," Nanny said. "Not many people can doctor a sick animal any better than you."

"Yeah, kind of in me I guess. Never know what a fellow might have turned out to be given half a chance."

The Old Man flicked ash from his cigarette into his pant cuff.

"Well, every day will be Sunday when they get the road fixed up." The glint in John's eyes brightened and a sardonic grin flitted across his face. "You must have seen the boys out with their telescope, or whatever they call it, and there's still a stake or two by the swamp bog from before the last election."

"How many elections does that make that they staked it off and still nothing done?"

John Cobly's grin went into a smile. He shook his head. "Can't remember that far back. We're just not voting the right way, I guess, Harv."

The Old Man's face shot full toward John. "They talking election again?"

"Never heard anything about it yet, but they could call one near as next fall. New government might do something, but the Liberals will probably go in again. Not that we don't need something decent. The whole bloody road is nothing but a swamp, you might as well say, spring and fall. Kills the heck out of a horse. Lose a horse, rig and all by the swamp bog.

"No doubt about that," The Old Man said. "But, oh well, we're getting by. Could be a lot worse, I guess."

"Things are going to have to change, though," John Cobly said. "More people going tractor these days and that road ain't no good for a tractor."

"I suppose that'll be the next thing. Think they're any good?"

"Oh yeah, they make a difference, work wise. You know yourself, Harv. A man can walk forty miles a day behind a plow, or a light harrows, keeping three ornery horses in line, when he could be riding along, sitting pretty. And them engines, Harv. You know yourself, they're up and down, choke a sheaf into a mill too fast, jam a log into a saw blade and they just about quit, and you have to wait on them to get up speed. Them little tractors just purr along like a kitten, steady as she goes."

"Yeah, I seen one in a mud hole on the way to town one day. Albert Champs, I think. It was purring pretty good, all right. Looked like it was trying to learn the foxtrot."

John Cobly sat bolt upright. "I'm talking about working the land. Just think of how much time you use up, harnessing and hitching. With a tractor, you just hook on when you want, no muss, no fuss, no manure, no feeding and resting. Keep the gas to her, change the oil now and then, a little grease, and she'll work all night if you want."

John Cobly took a last heavy drag from his cigarette butt and then went to the stove and poked it through a draft hole. He went back to the armchair, took a match from his pocket, flopped back down, and began digging wax out of his right ear with the match head.

"Still going to need a horse," The Old Man said. "How are you going to haul potatoes in the wintertime? They can't even keep the front road open with them truck affairs. The first couple of good storms, and roads like ours are choked up so bad in the cuttings they'd have to use a bulldozer in places."

"There's a new one coming out," John Cobly said. "Breaks in the middle. Fred James said he seen one up in Toronto at one of them shows for machinery, more engine than anything else. They'll be here before long."

"What's a tractor like with horse machinery?" The Old Man said.

"They're good, geared for them. Just cut off the poles and bolt on some kind of attachment for the draw bar—don't have to be fancy. Pretty much need a trip plow so you don't have to get off at the headland and put the shears in and out. Might as well throw in a blower attachment for your thresher. Thresh in the fall. Good idea to get a trailer, too."

The Old Man crushed out his cigarette butt between his thumb and forefinger and set it on the window ledge. "What do you need a trailer for?"

"Because they say it takes some kind of genius to back a wagon with one of those things."

"What else should you might as well get?"

John Cobly smirked. "That'll probably do for a start."

"For a start."

"Well, you know there's other things to make life easier. Hay loaders, tractor-built rakes and that."

"Yes, and where's all the money going to come from?"

"Banks are getting better these days with loans, Harv."

"What's a tractor go for?"

"Oh, fifteen hundred, give or take, for most all the little thirty-or-so horsepower tractors. They claim an extra acre of potatoes and a milk cow will keep up the payments."

"And what if the cow dies and the potatoes are worth nothing?"

"All part of farming, Harv. The whole thing's nothing but a gamble; you know that."

"Yeah, but there's such a thing as going out on a limb."

"Oh yeah, ain't that the truth. They're getting them, though, here and there. Seem happy enough with them. If they give us a decent road, it'll be tempting."

"Seems to me that tractors are for people like Fred James. Gone big enough to afford things without tick, got their own warehouses by the track and buying and shipping to boot. Seems to me, somewhere along the way, the bills are going to pile up more than we can handle."

"Ah, you're too set in your ways, Harv. Progress, Harv, progress— can't get in the way of progress. And that's how it should be. There are people right now, small farmers like us, think we're back in the stone age. The time for slaving and doing without is going to go."

The Old Man's face broke into a wry smirk.

"But we have to get the road fixed up first." John Cobly flashed his sardonic grin.

"No, first we'll have to vote the right way, then we just might get the road. We just might."

There was a pause. John Cobly's eyes shifted to me. "Well, Jake, feel like picking for me? I got work 'til Saturday depending on the weather. Feed you good, pay you on time, start you with a full section. Can't handle that, we'll give you a half. I'm a little short with them Cape Britoners gone."

"Might as well go ahead, Jake," The Boss said. "We can look after the barn work. Make a few bucks for yourself."

"He's a little young," Nanny said.

"Nah. It'll make a man of him."

"Okay," I said. "Give it a shot, anyway."

"That's the stuff," John Cobly said. There was another pause.

"How's your crop this year, John?" The Old Man said.

"Not bad, kind of small. Yours?"

"Not bad."

"What's a bushel worth now?"

"I heard thirty cents."

John shook his head. "Might as well leave them in the ground. What about beef?"

"Seventeen cents."

"Not that hot, either, eh?" John Cobly took out a match and worked the head around in his ear again, then took it out and flicked off the residue with his thumb. I've got two steers and a heifer to go. Couple of cattle buyers were around last week. Told them to come back after digging; figured the price might be half decent by then. Don't seem like a lot of hope."

"Pork's pretty good now," The Old Man said. "There's always something to prop things up. Sometimes I wonder if potatoes are worth bothering with, though. If you're not digging, you're grading and hauling, then you're planting, then you're roguing and spraying, then you're back to digging again."

"She's year round, all right. That's for sure. Lot of lifting and lugging, too. But nobody complains when the big prices hit. And they better hit me pretty soon."

"Maybe we should leave them alone altogether, like Dan."

John Cobly's eyebrows shot up. "But Dan is a walking miracle, no matter which way you look at things. How he manages things is a mystery. If he's not drinking, it seems, he's reading. I came by Sunday and he was standing out in the yard, two sheets in the wind. He wheeled around cross-legged, watching me go by. Don't think he knew what end of him was up. Still manages to get the work done, though, and his horses and stock are just strapping."

"When it comes to farming there's none better," The Boss said. "It's a delight to watch him plow, drunk or sober. He ever mention fixing up the porch anyways decent yet?"

"Hammered a shelf or two to the wall. Studs are still bare, though."

"Beer crock behind the stove, I suppose?"

"Oh yeah, you can count on that. And his books, that's what the shelves are for. Keeps his dishes in the oven."

"Come up with any new rhymes lately?"

"Probably has, but wouldn't let on. Get him at a tyme half lit and you never know what's going to come out of him."

"Better than what you'd hear on the radio, too."

"Oh yeah, radio can't hold a candle to Dan. And never cracks a smile. Makes it all the funnier."

"Must get down to see Dan; haven't seen him much lately.

He don't make a lot of sense when he's got a jag on, and he's pretty much had one on since the fire."

"I suppose you heard about the big wedding coming off," Nanny said.

"Yeah, Charlie is going to take the big leap. Agnes is taking up the collection and looking after the shower. We'll tamarack her down. It's coming off in June just after planting."

Nanny paused in her knitting and looked up. "What's she like, John?"

"Joanie Tripp? Seems like a nice young lady. Quiet. Her father got that store on Cobbler Road."

"Maybe she'll be too quiet for Charlie," Nanny said.

"Well, there's that. He's a corker, that fellow, especially when it comes to hockey and step-dancing; make a dog laugh, too."

"He was doing the barn work for us last winter when we were all down with the flu," The Old Man said. "He stuck his head in the door on his way home, the lugs of his cap up like wings, and them sharp eyes of his. 'Let me know if you decide to kill that red steer by the pig pen,' he said. 'He just about drove his foot through my rear end. I'd like to get first blow at him, help send him off.'"

"She might not be able to handle him, with his antics," Nanny said.

John Cobly chuckled. "You never know, though, about them women. They pretty well got a fellow figured out before they set their cap for him."

"And when they set their cap for a fellow, you might as well say he's done for," The Old Man said, eyeing Nanny.

Nanny's eyebrows shot up. Her needle clicks quickened. "I

suppose men don't set their caps for women," Nanny said.

"Not that I know of," The Old Man said.

"I guess maybe not. Pretty hard to set your cap and chase somebody at the same time." John Cobly's eyes gleamed, his face easing into a gleeful smirk.

"Maybe if you hadn't set your cap, you wouldn't have been chased," The Old Man said.

"I didn't have to set my cap to get chased."

"That's because you were chasing me."

"Keep talking like that, you old horse, and you'll get no lunch."

"The road of love is a rocky road," John Cobly said giddily.

"Now, you know you couldn't get along without me," The Old Man said.

"Can't get along without horses, either." Nanny's eyebrows had shot full height and the needles were clicking in high gear.

"She loves me, John, can't you tell?"

"Haven't the shadow of a doubt."

"Speaking of lunch," The Old Man said.

Nanny put down her knitting, moved to the stove and reached for the tea caddy in the warm closet.

"Don't be getting me any lunch, Ella," John Cobly said.

"Ah, you'll stay for lunch," The Boss said.

"You'll have to stay for lunch," Nanny said, pouring water into the teapot.

"Well…Agnes will be wondering, but, ah, I guess she won't mind. She put up with me this long, I guess she won't leave me if I don't get home right away."

There was a pause. I could hear Nanny bustling in the cupboard.

"Thinking of doing something with the school, Harv?"

"They're talking about it. But they've been talking about it since I got on the trustee's board. If they don't do something soon, the first thing you know the place will be in the cellar."

"Still talking about a furnace?"

"Once in a while. Talk about a lot of things. Bill spoke up the other night and said, 'It's about time we were thinking about getting running water and a flush toilet. It's a shame, them little ones freezing their backsides off all the time.' Clayton jumped in then: 'I never froze my backside off when I went to school,' he said. 'That's because you probably only went once a week,' Bill said."

"Haw, haw, haw," John Cobly belched out. "They'd be into it then."

"For at least half an hour. Would've been longer if old Harley hadn't jumped in: 'You bucks stop jawing and wasting time. Youse got more jaw than a government mule. We need to get a decent cellar under the place first, then a furnace so they won't be freezing their backsides off sitting in their seats.'"

"Sounds like when I was on the board; like pulling teeth, getting anything done," John Cobly said.

Nanny handed out our lunch plates and cups of tea and we took them on our laps and the conversation went on hold for a spell. A blow of wind buffeted the house. The burr of the fire stirred up briefly to fall with the wind.

John Cobly finally coordinated his tongue around heavy chews on a thick beef sandwich and tea slurps.

"I suppose you'll be out tricking pretty soon, Jake?"

"I don't play tricks," I said.

"Course not," The Old Man said.

"The young beggars turned my outhouse over last year," John Cobly said.

"I wouldn't know anything about that," I said.

"Course you wouldn't," The Old Man said. "Best way to beat them at that is to move the outhouse off the hole. Joe Chase…"

"Never mind, Harvey, were eating our lunch," Nanny said.

"I mind the time we took to work and hauled Wes Johnston's light wagon up onto his shed," John Cobly said. "Must have taken a couple of hours, us whispering and grunting and sweating. Just got it nicely sitting when he shined a flashlight on us. Wasn't the old beggar watching from the porch all the time! 'All right, boys; I know youse all, now take her down,' he said."

"Kind of turned the tables," The Old Man said.

"Told my old man, too. Kind of hard getting out of cleaning out the pigs after that, among other things."

"I guess we all had our day," The Boss said. There was a pause again with finishing lunch and replenishment of tea.

"By the way, how's your digger working, Harv?" John Cobly said.

"Better than a plow," The Old Man said.

"Did most of the digging yourself with them, all the clawing and scratching," John Cobly said.

"Yes, and the whirligigs send the potatoes halfway across the field," The Old Man said. "Instead of clawing and scratching, you're reaching after them."

"Yeah," John Cobly said. "I would have gotten an elevator if they were any good in wet and sod ground. Anyway, the reason I asked is because a claw on that old digger of mine got broke on a heavy stone. She still digs, but she smashes up the odd potato. I was wondering if I could get the lend of yours."

"Sure," The Old Man said. "Might need to throw a little grease at her."

"That'll be great. I'll just hook her onto me wagon on the way home."

The Old Man and John Cobly rolled a making apiece, lit up and settled back while Nanny collected the lunch dishes.

"Are they holding the tyme in the hall?" Nanny said from the pantry.

"No. George is going to straighten up the main floor in the old mill, him and Charlie."

"I thought Alf wasn't letting anybody near the old mill anymore," The Old Man said.

John Cobly chuckled with a belch of smoke.

"And him blacksmithing in the west side room with the roof half buckled in and the windows about to pop out. They were out in the yard a while back jawing over it. Alf just finished shoeing a horse for me. 'That place ain't fit for man nor beast,' George said. 'You just stick to your farming,' Alf said. 'Them fences ain't nothing to write home about, big mouth.'"

"Now George is going to hold a tyme in the main floor and Alf thinks it's too dangerous," The Old Man said. "Sounds like them."

"Charlie and Joanie going to move in?" Nanny said.

"Just 'til they get a piece built on."

"Poor Hilda," Nanny said. She was back at her knitting. "It would be something if Alf got a woman."

"Alf is too busy with his blacksmithing and inventing," John Cobly said.

"He takes after Willard," The Old Man said. "You'd go for grist and it would take half an hour to find him, then another half hour to get him away from something he was dreaming up. Remember the time he put the sail on the wood sleigh?"

"Yeah," John Cobly said. "Must have got her going fifty or more on a good crust of snow, with no way to steer it."

"No way to stop it either, but the woods did a pretty good job. Wonder he wasn't killed."

"Then he put the windmill on the pump in the barnyard."

"Yeah, gust of wind took it while he was gearing it up and the thing started chasing him across the barnyard. Just missed him, too. Hit the barn and tore off a big patch of shingles."

There was a pause.

"Don't seem long since Alf took over the mill," The Old Man said.

"Didn't run it long. Once the feed mill in town got underway and people started buying flour… Gorsh!" John Cobly stared at the clock. "Is that clock right? Is it really ten to nine? Agnes will skin me alive if I ain't home soon."

"Jake, take the flashlight and give John a hand with the digger," The Boss said.

"No need, Harv. I can hook her on. Not much of a trick."

"You sure?"

47

"Yeah, no trouble." John Cobly rose stiffly and stretched his stubby frame. "You and Ella will have to come over for a game of auction when things quiet down."

"I don't know. Might not be enough competition."

"Just youse come on over. I don't recall any Jackson ever giving me any trouble."

"We'll be over. We'll try not to trounce youse too bad."

"We'll be seeing you," John Cobly said. He paused with his hand on the doorknob and peered back at The Old Man. "Now remember to get ready to vote right, next election, so they'll fix up the road." He flashed another sardonic grin and left.

Prelude to Late Fall and Early Winter on Hook Road

When the potatoes were stowed and the binders and diggers were back in storage, the three-horse gang plows appeared along Hook Road, with the plowers limp-footing their way along, one foot on sod, the other in the groove of the over-turned furrow, sometimes taking their hands from the plow handles to saw on the reins looping their necks to check the horses or brush a run from their noses. While overhead, the grey-black clouds hovered in their slow, moody moil, adding their chill to the fall wind cuffing and furling the manes and tails of the horses and buffeting the circus of seagulls sweeping and banking and lighting to pick worms with quick pecks in the plows' wake.

A farmer was judged by his plowing. Indeed, if you could keep three horses in line enough to run a straight furrow, stones and rough ground considered, you were usually competent at everything else. The trick was to get the first run straight. The farmers would put something easily viewable, maybe a flour sack or an old shirt, on a post as a marker and proceed without taking their eyes off it.

Box carts appeared, too, their shafts riding high on the backs of the horses, and the farmers hoed out the cabbage, turnips, carrots and mangels, loaded them and carted them to their cellars. Then they forked and carted sod until the sod banks ringed the houses against the coming winter frost.

As late fall progressed toward early winter and what was left of pasture turned grey-brown and died, the calves and young cattle, half wild from pasture freedom, were driven, rope-hauled and tail-twisted into berths in the barns—except those selected to take a one-way trip on the truck of a cattle buyer. The stay of the one whose carcass would hang in any given woodshed for winter beef was somewhat shortened as well.

Then half molasses puncheons were filled with water heated in double boilers, kettles and pots on kitchen stoves, butchered pigs were block and tackle-hoisted by the pointed sticks in their hocks and dunked, and there was the steamy-acrid smell of pig, blood and hair during the scalding, the knife shaving and the junking for the barrels of brine.

Dan Coulter's battered saw gear, a two-by-four spiked angle-wise across its spindly front legs for support, made the rounds, and the stationary engines, poised like ducks to fly with their high pulley and balance wheels and nubbing water tanks, in their turn, were skidded from the barn floor, crowbarred into position a belt length from the saw and pegged down. The starting procedure was simple: adjust for spark, flip up the jigger on the oil glass by the water tank, then heave on the balance wheel until the machine's barks and sucks took hold and increased with the crank of the cylinder poking into its belly and the broad belt, soaped for traction, whirred and the machine resembled a rabid dog jigging and straining on a leash. Meanwhile, back at the saw gear, the thump of the first log on the worn, gouged table broke into the whispering hum of the saw's talon-toothed circular blade and the shuttle of its frame.

A swipe at the safety lever protruding above the table's back, by the blade slot, a straight-armed, brace-legged push on the log toward the whispering hum, and the saw gear symphony began: the quickening of the engine barks, which become laboured with the run-down mourn of the blade cutting through, the cling of the blade dinging the severed block with the table's return, the clop of the block—heaved by the blocker—hitting the frozen ground, the engine barks spacing in runaway momentum, the thumps of the log bounced up for the next cut. And there were the baked smells of hot sawdust, and dirty water boiling in the engine's belly.

When the twenty or so cords of rock maple and beech peaked in their piles, a snugness settled over the people of Hook Road, a slowdown came and they moved as those who had conquered another hard season as they waited for the first big snow storm. It came in mid-December, blocking the road with heavy drifts.

Then, in keeping with time-worn tradition, they took to their wood sleighs with sets of wire-cutter/pliers and brush for markers, and, taking the path of least snow resistance, each farmer in his own allotment, they broke the winter road.

And it wound, resembling twin snakes following a shallow ditch pitted by horse hooves and peppered by horse buns. Across open fields, twisting and turning to avoid the heavier drifts, through fences with cut wire furling back, through yards and ditches and sometimes on the road, it wound, its ragged brush markers stating its course. In its run, where it crossed the lesser banks, which in themselves could be formidable, jolting pitches formed from the rock and ram of sleigh runners, making for a precarious ride.

There was also a bit of the precarious in the fact that there was only one trail for two-way traffic. There were road rules, of course. Empty and full sleighs meeting got a track apiece; an empty sleigh gave right of way to a full sleigh; a sleigh passing from the rear, empty or full, got a wave. Misdemeanours were punished by name-calling and expenditure of smashed sleigh sides and broken runners.

Late Fall and Early Winter on Hook Road

CHAPTER 3

Wally Mason and I made our musical debut at the Christmas concert that year. The whole thing came about in the way peculiar to endeavours that have no real direction. The course of things began the previous summer, when a country music show came to town. The fiddler they had stacked up with the best. Segments of the show were aired over the local radio station. Wally Mason got inspired and dug an old fiddle and bow out from the attic.

They could have belonged to a grand-uncle, but nobody knew for sure. Neither was much to brag about—maybe fifteen hairs left in the bow, and they had to be knotted, there was such a wow in the shaft. The fingerboard had finger-worn patches and the strings—mostly of gut—were dirt-stiff and blackened. But it was sound enough to tune and Jim Mackie set it up and gave Wally a few basic lessons.

Joe Mason's farm was directly across from ours, with the same frontage running down to Tom Dougal's line. There was Joe and his wife, Mabel, his daughter, Jenny, and son, Wally, who was around my age and a little younger than his sister. Wally and I pretty much grew up together: played together, fought together, went to school together; he was the closest thing to a brother I would ever have.

I came into the Masons' yard one evening not long after Wally started into the music. Joe was standing by their porch door, short, bandy-legged and belligerent. He was thrusting his arm toward the barn with cants of his cannonball head, his word phrases coming in shots: "Get to the barn with that thing, go up loft, scare all the rats out of the granary they'll think twenty seven mad cats and a drunken piper is out to get them, and don't squawk that thing when the milk cows are around, they'll not let down their milk for a month." Wally came out then, his long, skinny legs dragging his oversized feet in his waggling shuffle. There was a sulky scowl on his long, thin face, made sharper by a long, thin nose. Of course, he had "that thing" under his arm.

In any given evening after that, you could find Wally perched on a loft girder in the barn, sawing away, staring in concentration, his tongue lolling out and his jaw working to the dip and saw of the bow.

I'd sit on the girder and watch for a while. Eventually he'd pause, take a quick look at me and say, "Now tell me what this one is, Jake." And he'd saw away with his eyes staring at me.

I'd make a few guesses when he'd finish and his eyes would go blank in their stare. Then he'd shake his head in disgust.

"You don't have much of an ear for music if you can't even tell what that is, Jake," he'd say. But one evening I caught the second half of "Saint Anne's Reel" over and over with Wally sitting smug-faced and his jaw clamped shut. He didn't have much time for me that night.

The next evening, I was sitting on a stone by Alban Gallant's door with his old, neck-sprung guitar, learning chords.

Alban's gateway was pretty much dead across from John Cobly's. His frontage, like John's, ran down to the Wallace's line, which was about two hundred yards from their farm buildings and the mill by the creek. Alban and his wife, Annette, had seven children, like the steps of stairs, and the whole family was musical. They were standard entertainment at the tymes and Alban accompanied Jim Mackie on guitar as well.

Alban was moving some pigs from pen to pen and he pretty well taught me between pigs, leaning over me—with that pig smell from the odd patch of manure on his overalls—to place my fingers on the strings. I got the D, A and G chords down half decent by the time he got the pigs settled in. "Now practise them chords," Alban said. "Over and over. Then practise changing from one to the other. Then start humming a tune while you strum and change chords. You got any ear at all, it'll tell you when it sounds right. Same with the fiddle. You want to tune to the fiddle, use this third string with the second one on the fiddle. Here you go. Keep the guitar long as you want. It's good enough to learn on. I got me a Gibson." A slightly bemused look came into his round-set eyes and over his square, Acadian face with its jaw jut. "You hit the big time, I want your autograph," he said.

A few evenings later, I showed up at Joe Mason's barn loft. Wally paused, eyeing me with the bow dead on the strings. Then he sawed a few notes looking at the straw; then he eyed me again, sideways, and lifted the bow. "Figured we could work her together," I said. "Alban taught me." I whistled "Home on the Range" and worked the chords.

"But that ain't 'Saint Anne's Reel,' Jake."

"Figured we could work that out between us."

"You're going to tie me up and slow me down, Jake."

"You're going to have to learn to play with a guitar sooner or later."

Wally canted his head and studied the straw again.

It took a while to persuade him, but we finally got at it. We managed to get tuned and away in some kind of recognizable gnash. Probably nobody could call it music, except us, and that only by spells. But we sawed and flailed away, fought a few times, quit twice. But there's an element in learning that holds back the whole truth, at least there was in our case, and we worked away at it pretty much the rest of the summer. It's only proper to mention that Joe Mason never went near the barn on any given evening that summer for no good reason.

We eased off a bit during grain harvest and potato digging. Partly because of the work and partly because we had pretty much wore out our version of "Saint Anne's Reel." We tried "Nelly Grey" and "Red Wing" and a few like that, but Wally didn't take to them all that good.

"They're not really tunes, Jake," Wally said. "Anybody can play them; got to have a little class, too, you know."

And we can handle all the class we can get, I thought, but I kept that one to myself. We'd had a pretty good row the night before. By the time the cold began to pick up and we were spending most of our time blowing on our fingers, we decided to pack it in. I left the guitar at the Masons' hoping things would resume somehow, but after a couple of weeks with nothing happening, I decided I might as well go one evening and take it home.

Joe Mason gave me an owly look when I stepped inside the door. "He's in the attic," he said. "Make sure you keep the door shut."

Wally was playing by candlelight, perched on an old trunk with his back to the brick flue, which took most of the heavy off the cold. Around him, the hat racks, bedspring, broken desk, bottles and junk known to old attics cast their shadows on the wall and what bareness there was on the floor. He was sawing away on "The Barley Corn Reel," a new tune I'd heard on the radio a few weeks back. He was clamp-jawed with that smug look again. He just glanced my way, then stared straight ahead and kept driving 'er. But he had my guitar leaning on an overturned orange crate, so I got set up and tried to flail in, but there was no way.

"Hey, wait a minute, wait a minute," I said. "How are you playing that? I can't follow you at all."

Wally paused, peering down his nose at me with the bow horizontal on the strings. "That's how it was played on the radio; I picked it off the radio," Wally said, smirking in his smugness.

"But I can't follow you."

"There's more than three chords in this game, Jake. You want to play with me you'll have to learn them."

"Let's go to Jim Mackie's some night and get him and Alban to iron things out for us?"

"There's always that possibility," Wally said, sawing away again. Eventually, he paused, peered sideways at me, and smirked again. "Great to be smart, ain't it, Jake," he said.

We didn't have to make any arrangements. Any evening Jim and Alban had nothing better to do, which was most of the time, they'd be at Jim's going over tunes.

We went on an evening just after the first early snow. There were smatterings of drifted snow on the road and our footsteps rattled on the frozen wheel ruts. The night was dead quiet with the gloom of a moonless, winter blackness that would augment at the bark of a distant dog.

Jim Mackie's farm was on the east side of the road, facing Dan Coulter's property. Both farms ran from the hollow down to the creek. We could hear the rhythmic gnash of fiddle-guitar music when we passed the woods of spruce on the crown of the hollow's north bank, and when we came around the wood house, just at the gate, we could see Jim's head weaving with the music and the jiggle and dip of his bow arm in the inverted V of the curtains of his kitchen window.

Jim's wife, Alice, and daughter, Shirley—both plump, black-haired and round faced, looking more like sisters—were playing forty-fives at the kitchen table. They answered in chorus to our knock above the music and greeted us between card slaps as we entered. The music stopped suddenly. Jim and Alban nodded at us in greeting, then sat eying us curiously.

"I hear you boys are into the music these days," Jim Mackie said. "Let's see your stuff." He held out his fiddle and bow to Wally.

Alban Gallant held out his guitar to me.

It took Wally a bit of anxious juggling—getting his mitts in his pocket, then his coat off, working the bow and fiddle from hand to hand—and me about the same with the guitar, but we finally got set and into "The Barley Corn Reel." Jim Mackie quietly studied Wally while he played, his dark eyes peering from his square face, which was brightened by a fringe of steel-grey hair, and his stout arms folded across his chest.

"Sounds like 'The Barley Corn Reel,'" Jim said when we stopped. "You're in the sharps and flats."

"I learned it from the radio," Wally said. He was holding Jim's fiddle and bow with some kind of reverence.

Jim took them and began sawing segments of the tune in that halt of learning until he paused with the bow on the strings and snap-canted his head.

"I'll be danged," he said. "I've been trying to get that one down for weeks and you just gave me the gist of it in the right key. If you picked that off the radio, you've got an ear for music; I'll tell you that right now."

"I want to be an Old Tyme Fiddle Champion," Wally said. He was bending toward Jim with that reverence shining in his eyes.

"Think you'll make 'er, do you?" Jim Mackie said, his eyes in a thoughtful peer. "Well, you never know." He went back to working the tune.

"And you don't know the chords," Alban Gallant said, looking at me. I nodded. Alban took the guitar, his left hand taking position. "You use bar chords," he said. He ran his left hand up the neck of the guitar, shifting his fingers and barring chords. He paused now and then, watching Jim, waiting for a chord turn in his fiddling. "A sharp," Alban Gallant finally said, holding up his left index finger. "You use this finger instead of the nut—that's this white thing here at the end of the fingerboard. You use the other fingers to get the chord, like this…" He paused for a minute with his fingers on the strings, thinking. "Wait a minute; got any elastic?" he said to no one in particular.

"Take one of the wife's garters," Jim Mackie said, without a pause.

"I use binder twine—all I can afford," Alice said, slapping down the pack of cards. "Hearts are trump."

"Enough to tie up a good-sized sheaf, too," Jim said.

"And enough to hang you with," Alice said. She lurched out of her chair then, slapping down her cards, and got a piece of white elastic from the radio shelf. She dropped it on Alban on her way back to sit down.

"Where did you get that?" Jim Mackie said.

"Never you mind."

Alban Gallant took half a pencil from his pocket and constructed a crude capo by choking the guitar neck with the elastic and binding the tips of the pencil with it laying across the strings. "You make up one of these and put it where you get the right sound with the chords, you know, see?"

"Yeah, I do," I said. I took the guitar and moved the capo up and down the strings, working my three chords, marvelling at how such a complicated thing could be made so simple.

"Time you learned a few more," Alban said after watching me awhile. "Here." He began placing my fingers on the strings. "This is C... This is F... You use them with G... Yeah, good. You learn quick."

Jim Mackie had not paused in his pondering saw.

"He's into it," Alice said, eyeing Jim and slapping down a card. "There'll be nothing but squeaks and squawks tonight. Once he starts a tune, he's gone."

Jim paid Alice no heed.

Alban Gallant paused, watching Jim with a smirk on his face. "Well I guess I'll head home," he said. He paused again, still looking at Jim. Finally, he took the guitar, deconstructed the capo, and put the guitar in a homemade canvas bag.

"Don't forget to give the elastic back to the wife," Jim Mackie said, deadpan. "It might belong to her 'unmentionables.'" He did not pause in his fiddling.

"I use binder twine for them, too," Alice said.

"We'll be seeing youse," Alban said, heading for the door.

Everybody responded but Jim.

"You boys may as well join us in a four-hander of Auction," Alice said.

We sat in and played three games and Jim never let up. We had lunch and Jim didn't even let up to eat; his tea went cold beside the sandwiches and cake in a saucer on the stove's oven door.

"If I was a squeeze box, he would have traded me in for a fiddle by now," Alice said when we left.

Jim managed a "keep at her" without breaking stride.

Outside, the night had grown gloomier, speaking of more snow. There was still no wind. We walked in silence down past Dan Coulter's house, which was situated just below the crown of the hollow. The shallow lamp glow from Dan's window stretched our shadows angle-wise and cast a faint glow at the block of woods by the brook as we made our way along.

"If I get a decent price for my muskrat pelts, I should be able to get a new Harmony guitar from the catalogue," I said.

"Let me know when you order," Wally said. "I'll get a new set of strings and a bow and maybe a junk of rosin." Suddenly he jig-skipped and sang out: "Here we go, Fiddling Wally Mason and Picking Jake Jackson with 'The Barley Corn Reel.' And he diddled into the tune and I joined in with a wing-wang, wing-wang and broke into a jig-skip, too.

We were still jig-skipping, diddling and wing-wanging when we got to Wally's gate and I could hear his jig-skips and hey-diddle, harrough-a-diddle down his lane right up until his door slammed shut.

The Boss was sitting with his ear to the radio when I came in. The words, coming through the usual buzz, were rising and lowering sporadically, sometimes cutting out: "Vital...at Holl...into the boards...sin bin...Gre...up centre to...Bou... y...Pitsod...out...Whitlo...scores! They don't call him...is... lighter...for nothing." Everything blanked out into a buzz then.

"What's the score?" I asked.

"Five–two, Halifax. Charlottetown forgot to get out of bed."

The Boss fished into his pocket for a fifty-cent piece and held it out to me. "Get a dry-cell tomorrow," he said.

"Did you try heating the old one?"

"You can. I'm going to bed."

After he left, I unhooked the cylinder-like battery behind the radio and sat it on the stove's oven door for the night. By the shallow light from the kitchen, I poured a glass of milk from the porch bucket and used a butcher knife to cut a chunk off the boiled tongue curled on a plate on a side shelf. Then I went to the pantry and made a sandwich with the tongue and Nanny's freshly baked bread and sat and ate with my feet on the stove's oven door, savouring the crunchy bread crust mingling with the tongue and the milk, hearing the low whine of the kettle and the odd snap from the firebox. When I finished, I groped up the stairs through the cold darkness and got my slingshot.

Back at the stove, I cut one of the bicycle tube pulls off the slingshot and geared up a capo on the guitar and slid it up and down the neck, working chords for a while. Before the fire died and the kitchen got cold, I went and got the catalogue and turned to the page where the Harmony guitar stood in stateliness and mystery beside its case.

I really didn't have to go to the catalogue to see the guitar; it had been fixed in my mind for well over a month. When I trudged through my potato-picking stint for John Cobly; when I approached the brook in the early morning darkness listening for splashes around the trap area; when I skinned a muskrat by lantern light in the shop with the sour burnt kerosene smell mingling with that of the musky, raw carcass;

when I rolled a pelt inside out onto a pointed board, nailed it on and scraped off the lumps of fat; when I mailed the silky-haired, stiff hides wrapped in heavy, brown paper tied with binder twine, that guitar hung in the back of my mind like a vision.

It all came together a few weeks later, when The Old Man picked Wally and me up after school with the wood sleigh and pointed to a hump in the buffalo at the bottom of the sleigh. "There's a dangerous machine in there I got at the post office. Better wait 'til you get home to find out what it is. The frost won't do it any good."

Then there was that awe and excitement of opening the triangular box in the kitchen, smelling the fresh newness of the guitar and holding it. Wally's bow, strings and rosin were strategically placed inside the box. He grabbed them like a starving cat and disappeared.

But he was back that evening. I was too wrapped up in my new guitar to go over. He had his fiddle, with the new strings on, new bow, rosin and all, in a potato sack.

"Going to try some potato music, are youse," The Old Man said. He was laying on the couch smoking his pipe and peering over his glasses with a wry look.

"Let's see what youse can do. How about 'Saint Ann's Reel'?"

"I'm a little cold right now," Wally said.

"Good way to thaw out your fingers."

We got set up and Wally got off after a few false scrapes with me flailing away best I could with the lice comb I was using as a pick. The pick Alban Gallant gave me broke and it hadn't dawned on me that I could have gotten a bunch for ten cents when I ordered the guitar. When we stopped we sat looking at The Boss like two hounds hoping for a bone. We couldn't tell much by his expression; he had his hand over his mouth. When he finally took his hand away, he had a bemused smirk.

"Not bad," he said. "Youse could pretty well tell what youse were trying to play."

"As if he'd know," Nanny said, her knitting needles clicking, "the old goat. Youse sounded lovely. Youse should get in on the school concert. They'd love to have you."

"Think so?" Wally said.

"Sure."

"Think we could have a tune in your parlour, just this once, Mrs. Jackson?"

"Sure. The Queen Heater is lit. It'll be nice and warm."

"Go into the little room at the side; leave the door ajar," The Boss said.

We hadn't really considered the Christmas concert before that. But by the time Wally went home we were sold on it. With our new equipment, we thought ourselves quite the professionals and we went at it pretty well every night right up to when they started practising for the concert.

It was customary for the teacher to begin giving the concert assignments—the skits, songs and whatever—amidst the daily lessons at school. We worked so much each day until the last two weeks, when we took everything to the hall full-time right up to the big day.

Our teacher had that up-beat exuberance all teachers seem to have when we approached her. "Bring your instruments," she said. Next day, she set us up front by the blackboard with everyone else watching stiff, still and big-eyed. Of course, Wally was set on 'The Barley Corn Reel,' or the gist of it, which was no doubt somewhat less than we imagined. Wally's bow arm locked right off, making the bow veer at angles. His jaw and tongue were working kind of out of sync, too. But we worked away, finally locking into some semblance of music.

Most of the class, including the teacher, had their hands over their mouths, and some were bucking at the shoulders. They managed to hold back, though, except Gail Macdonald. Johnny Hately caught her arm and jerked her hand away from her mouth and she let out a yelp.

"Give them a hand," the teacher said when we finished. She had to choke out the words. She didn't take long getting us into our lessons.

Every so often, pretty well right up until recess, the odd person would be seized with shoulder bucks, taking sneak peeks at us with a hand over his or her mouth. At recess, with strained composure, the teacher told us to just practise at home until we moved to the hall.

On our way outside I said, "Wally, I've been meaning to tell you something. You know, your tongue lolls out and your jaw works sometimes when you play."

"They do?"

"Yeah." Wally gave me a dour look. In the yard, on two opposite snowbanks, divided by a large dip, most everybody else was forming up in two opposing lines for a snowball fight. "That's got nothing to do with the music."

"But it looks funny."

"Ah, go on," Wally snarled.

He went and stood by himself by the side of the school and waited until I picked a side and took the other.

"Let's get Jackson!" Wally yelled and I was hit with a hail right off the top.

The battle was on then, and it raged, with the smacked crossing to the opposite side until one side gained the upper hand through attrition. Finally, Urban Gallant stood alone, jumping, dodging, slipping and kicking up his feet, with an all-out volley zeroing in until he suddenly turned into a leopard. Then we had an all-out, pelt-in-your-face, throw-down-your-neck tangle. And there was Wally at close quarters, lining me up, with his mouth open—and I half crammed, half threw in a loose gob of dirty slush. We went home in different sleighs that afternoon.

I didn't know whether I should go to the Masons' that night or not, but I wound up going. Wally was sitting on the stove tank whittling on a stick, scowling with his jaw jutting out. He didn't speak, didn't even look at me.

I talked awhile with Joe about the weather. Mabel was sewing a patch to the seat of a pair of overalls, her long fingers working the needle and thread, her thin shoulders slightly hunched, a set of square glasses perched on the end of her long, pointed nose. Jenny, who I found pretty in a skinny sort of way, with her pert nose, long, red hair and blue eyes, did her homework at the table as if I didn't exist and never would.

I kept eyeing Wally, sizing him up before I spoke. I finally took a chance. "Well, Wally, going to have a tune?" I said.

He didn't answer; just went on whittling. I waited. Finally, he climbed off the tank and shuffled toward the door to the attic stairs. "You coming?" he grumped, halfway to the door.

We were barely getting started when Wally stopped and said, "You're out of tune."

"You're still sore about what I said, ain't you?"

"Ain't sore about nothing. Get in tune." We went through the tuning for a while, the plunks of the fiddle and the up and down wings of the guitar strings augmenting the gloom of the shadows on the wall, the feeble candlelight hitting the side of Wally's face, making his scowl grotesque. After he hitched around a bit, we finally started off.

There are times in learning activity, music or whatever, when things just hit home. Maybe it was because Wally was miffed and forgot himself; maybe it was incentive brought on by the upcoming concert; maybe it was just timing. Whatever the case, for two star-gazers in Joe Mason's attic that night, their lips blue and their fingers stiffening with the cold, things hit home and "The Barley Corn Reel," though not in the full sail of a schooner, at least in the steady chop of a row boat, took off. I'd say the continuation record for "The Barley Corn Reel," with Wally sawing away, his jaw set firm, a devious, victorious glint in his eye, and me dinging my best, was eternally broken.

When we finally stopped, Wally blew on his fingers and said, "We ain't doing nothing but 'The Barley Corn Reel' right up to the concert."

I held my fingers over the candle. "Wouldn't it be safer to go with 'Saint Anne's Reel'?" I said.

"Nope, not fancy enough."

"We better go another round and get out of here before we

freeze up solid."

"Okay," Wally said, with the fiddle under his chin again. "Here we go. Old Tyme Fiddle Champ, Fiddling Wally Mason with Picking Jake Jackson: 'The Barley Corn Reel.'"

The first day at the hall, we were an entity unto ourselves, as far as we were concerned: sitting by the pot-bellied stove, glowing red around its ring, and listening to the older girls harmonizing "Noël" on the short steps leading to the stage, Bob Scovie's random plunks at the keys of the piano standing kitty-corner to the stairs, and now and then the rattle of hard coal scuttling into the stove and the door shutting to the clang of the coal scoop—all echoing in the high-ceilinged room smelling of old varnish, burning coal dust and must.

Jackie Wall just about got things going right off. He was flapping his arms and crowing like a rooster at centre stage and a poke from behind the curtain knocked him off. He hit the floor with a *ka-thump* and came barrelling at us. He just missed the chair Wally had laid his fiddle on in a potato sack. It took me and the teacher and a couple of others a while to keep Wally from going at him with the coal scoop.

Except for our rehearsal as two dumb shepherds, we sat by the stove, with Wally burning his initials into a scrap of board with a hot poker. He had a sober, determined look on his face, sitting there with a twist of smoke curling past his ear.

When our time came, the teacher got us set up on stage with the air of someone who would just as soon do something else. The rest of the class sat up close in the chairs as if this was something not to be missed. But Wally kicked in big time, with a glaring stare, getting a fair junk of the tune and the rhythm— no tongue loll, his jaw set.

Everyone, including the teacher, stared with his or her mouth open. I had to kick Wally's chair and knock him off key to get him to stop; he must have went ten turns. The teacher had her hand flat on her face. "My," she said, after a dead silence. "My, my, my. Well, I guess we'll try the tea skit. I guess you boys can just keep practising until the concert, at home on your own."

Wally peered sidewise at me when we got back to the stove. "We showed them owl hoots a thing or two," he said.

For the rest of the time, we went through the rerun lines of skits and solos, in that halting try-again manner, with the teacher's patient prompting, spaced by the bumps and scrapes of the old sofa, table, chairs and back wall arrangements. Outside of our shepherd stints, Wally sat beside me at the stove in supreme smugness. I guess you could say we both sat that way.

The big day finally came. The trustees hauled in the tree, with its fresh, septic smell, and we dragged the big cardboard box of decorations down from the attic, decorated the tree and nailed up wreaths and bows.

Wally and I didn't bother to go home for supper; we came in the morning wearing our good clothes, with a few extra sandwiches in our lunch cans so we could rehearse with the place to ourselves.

The place looked magical and cozy now, with tiny, coloured lights peeping among the wreaths frilling the cut-out "Merry Christmas" at the jaw of the stage, and the decorations on the tree: the raining icicles, silver sprig lines, coloured balls and crepe ropes.

I can't remember the like ever happening, but if a thief had plied his trade in the district on concert night, he would have done well.

Only the sick, infirm and the odd person with some kind of grump didn't attend. They came singular and in groups, in overcoats and buckle overshoes, with that quiet, wondering expression reserved mostly for church and funerals. And they squatted to the chairs, glancing around and murmuring barely above a whisper, sometimes moving to a better viewing site.

Except for when we trooped on stage for the opening chorus to the piano plunks of "Marching to Georgia," and our shepherd stint at the nativity scene, when my beard came unstuck and I had to hold it to with my hand, we sat and watched the others as they wobbled their way through, taking nervous glances at the audience sitting in semi-darkness, intent on catching every word, be it choked, flubbed or stammered.

Our time came after the intermission and the hard fudge sale, when the usual lump or two rattled off the walls and the odd bald head while Jim Mackie and Alban Gallant played a few reels and the Gallant children stepped her off.

We made our way to the two chairs set up for us at centre stage. Wally's movements were quick and deliberate, his eyes like burning coals. He cut in before the teacher finished her introduction. We were pretty well into the tune before they got the curtain up.

I guess you could say the inevitable happened then. Although I don't think it would have if they'd given us more time to rehearse. It was kind of like getting hit with a bucket of cold water when you're not expecting it. That dry, deserted feeling grabbed me and froze me up, knocking me off stride; it grabbed Wally at about the same time and everything flopped into squawks and offbeat guitar dings.

Wally kept at it though, kept working away with his bow arm locked. Then I saw his jaw start to work. Then his tongue lolled out and he bit down on it with it still a ways out and still trying to work. When I looked at the crowd, the few faces I could see had an awestruck look. Then it was like something simmering into blowing up until we were hit by a gale of laughter that came in a belch. I glanced to the off-stage corner and saw the teacher standing with her shoulders bucking, her face beet red and her lips pursed shut. But Wally limped away, with me getting a ding in now and then. I was worried he might bite off his tongue. The roar of laughter carried on for some time after they dropped the curtain on us, with Wally still working away like he was trying to catch up.

In the end he stomped backstage, stiff-necked and with his peculiar belligerence. "I ain't playing no more," he said. "Laugh at a fellow like that."

Over in a corner, behind one of the movable back walls, Linda Robbins and Janet Fuller were waiting for their skit. Janet was finding it hard to keep a straight face, but Linda came over with something akin to sympathy in her blue eyes and on her plump face, framed by blonde curls. "That's okay, Wally," she said. "You gave it your best and you did a good job."

That wasn't much help, since even he knew he didn't.

Wally went and hid in the basement right up until the closing chorus and he wasn't too fussy about coming out then, but the teacher coaxed him to it. Trouble was, when everyone saw him again, there was another belch of laughter. He stood singing with a shoulder hitched up and his head canted like a dog in the rain. Then he realized he was the centre of attraction, and his face lost its stiff twist. He squared off to the audience with his head back, and the roar got louder.

I guess if Santa hadn't come about then, they'd have laughed until they got home. But he came, ho, hoing his way in from the cold. He went through his usual greeting, then handed out the gifts—prearranged by the hat raffle—amidst that bluster and excitement brought on by presents, the giving and receiving.

They kind of lost it again when Santa dealt Wally his. "Ho, ho, ho, to fiddling Wally Mason from someone who cares. Now I wonder who that could be?"

When everything was all over and we were getting on our overcoats and overshoes in the buzz and muddle, big Stewart Lucas, with his paunch bulging from his open overcoat, his open overshoes flapping, his piano key teeth going from ear to ear in his big, round face, came and said, "Wally, I never thought you had it in you. To put on a show like that must have taken some doing. And Jake, that get up you had on your guitar made it all the funnier."

The Old Man and Nanny went home just after we played. One of the milk cows had bloated that afternoon and John Cobly had to come over and tap her. They wanted to get home and keep an eye on her. I went home with the Masons.

It was a cold, dark night. There was a slight wind, but you could still hear the squeak and crunch of sleigh runners amidst the bumps at the pitches, coming in ragged cadence along the string of rigs, with the surprised yelps and laughter. Wally and I weren't laughing, though. We rode in glum silence.

The Boss was sitting by the radio listening to Inspector Faraday wedge out a grudging "Merry Christmas" to Boston Blackie.

He eyed me sideways with a smirk on his face before breaking into a full smile. I put my guitar away, then sat with my feet on the oven door and drank a cup of the hot chocolate Nanny had left simmering on the back of the stove when she went to bed. When the program finished, The Old Man told me to take a look at the sick cow before I went to bed and turned in himself.

I usually stayed up late on Christmas Eve, but I felt like going to bed early. My musical dreams had taken a licking, to say the least. Buying my new guitar didn't seem like such a good idea now. I put my clothes on and got the flashlight. When I got to the heavily iced doorstep, I paused and looked up. A few stars had broken through. There was a quiet stillness disturbed mildly by the raucous bark of a fox and a crump from cracking ice in a distant field. I could see the glow of lights from the city off to the north and, as if by some cue, the northern lights began to flare and dance from beyond.

In the stable, the sick cow's eyes showed blank, white circles in the light when she turned them to me from where she lay. I could hear the snuffs of her breathing mingling with the cud chews of the other cows and their chain rattles. The tap affair protruding from her side showed no signs of escaping gas and her belly was not barrelling. She snuffed again curiously, then turned her head away peacefully and chewed her cud.

I had left the radio on, and when I got back to the bask of light strewing from the kitchen window across the pitted foot path in the snow, I could hear one of the big bands with that mellow horn gnash playing "Silent Night." I paused, noticing the peaceful stillness, and watched the northern lights over the city lights again.

Inside, the usual whine of the kettle, the odd crack from the stove's firebox, the lamp's glow and the shadows on the wall all seemed to augment the music of Christmas coming from the radio. I sat in the armchair by the radio with another cup of hot chocolate. A mixed choir began singing a carol medley, giving background music while a lady narrated the Christmas story. When they finished, I worked my way—winging and wooing—through the stations, fielding carols. The stations were beginning to blank out by the time the heat from the stove had begun to die away and I was pleasantly tired. I took the lamp and went into the living room and looked at the small tree, modestly dressed with the winds of red and green crepe rope with their squished spaces, the paint-peeled coloured bells and balls, the pigs' hair icicles, the crockery angel on the top sprig with her wand and the jagged hole in her dress. I hung my sock on the mantel, reaching over the line of Christmas cards waggling wing-like in the heat waves from the Queen Heater burning below. Of course I didn't believe in Santa Claus anymore; it was just a part of Christmas I still enjoyed with Nanny. I paused for a few moments, feeling the mirth-like coziness brought together by the spruce and burnt maple smells, and as I went to bed I knew that tomorrow would be Christmas, and it would have that specialness it always had, musical dreams or no musical dreams.

I woke early, like always, and got the sock from the mantel; like always, it had an orange, that hard, smooth candy in animal shapes, a couple of striped canes and a handful of grapes. And like always, it was special.

The day broke fine and clear. There was a cold, bright freshness in the morning when the animals traipsed to the ice-bearded watering trough, with its axe-chipped hole. The steers rammed their heads into the snow like playful children blanking their faces white, their breath puffs seemingly coming from the snow. There was still a cold, bright freshness when Aunt Laura and Uncle Jim and their twin boys rode in from town in their pung sleigh with bells jingling.

It was nice sitting around the kitchen amidst the Christmas dinner smells, going through the usual greetings, exchanging gifts and showing them off, finally eating goose, mashed potatoes and jimmies, topped off with plum pudding to the point of a groan. Then we sat and listened to Uncle Jim tell about town goings-on, and him discussing politics with The Boss while The Boss whittled a plunger for a cut goose quill so the children could shoot potato plugs. But I had other things on my mind.

I stuffed my pockets with lumps of fudge and the hard candy from my sock, grabbed my new fleece-lined leather mitts from under the tree and headed for the porch. I threaded my hockey stick through the spaces in my skates and swung them over my shoulder. There was a steady drip from the icicles on the eaves of the porch; a few drops fell down my neck as I stepped out into the cold, bright freshness again.

Across the sparkling fields of snow, I could see the banks of the cleared ice patch below Joe Mason's house rising above the white glare. Wally, hidden below the knee, was skating limp-legged and laboured. He was pushing a board nailed to a two-by-four, with support sticks, for a scraper.

Jenny and Shirley Mackie were on the ice, too, skating straight-backed, straight-armed and tottery, sweeping in a forward slant, taking a stride and daring to take another, coasting for the rump-waggling, sidewise stop, with... *whoops!...there goes Jenny!*

As I trudged with my feet plunging through soft-crusted snow, I saw others come wading, their breaths puffing and swirling around their faces and cap lugs.

We came to sit on our sticks, with their rags of tape at the blade. We blew on our chilled fingers between the tightening of waxed laces and the usual hockey banter. Finally we rose like wounded birds scattering from a roost with the ever-present stick for support. Then it was pick sides, drop the puck and drive 'er, with spaced boots for nets, no refs and no offsides. And there were the rip and swish of rust-pitted blades cutting and swerving, the whacks of clashing sticks, the cheers of the score. And somewhere outside the white banks, the cares and defeats of life skulked like defeated dogs, and until early winter shadows grew long before distant trees, the world was on hold.

The banter was somewhat subdued as we sat on our sticks again. Steam wisps rose from our hands as we pried the laces loose from their castings of sprayed ice and hauled off the skates and stuffed our feet into stiff boots where they would grow hot. Feeling the ice strange to our feet without the fight for balance, we said our "see yas" and saw the first flickers of lamps in distant windows punctuating the peace of Christmas night.

Prelude to Winter on Hook Road

From the first big storm, except for the hockey, skating and coasting circuses, the scenes along Hook Road pretty much included a horse and sleigh. In milder days—after limp-foot lugging seventy-five– or one hundred-pound bags of Green Mountains or Sebagos up the stone steps of gloomy cellars— the farmers rocked and swayed with the pitches, perched on the buffalo-covered wood sleigh loads, sometimes in a string.

At mid-afternoon, on sleighs returning from the potato buyers, the scholars of the old schoolhouse rode, perched on sleigh sides like multi-coloured birds chirping on telephone lines. And there were songs in chorus and jokes, which sooner or later evolved into push-offs and laughing and foot-skipping races to catch up, with slung school bags swinging in flurries of flying snow until the driver's rein slapped the horses into a jog, resulting in pushing, foot-slipping, laughing races to catch up. And sometimes a speed comment from a passing sleigh would bring on a foot race, and the cheers and jeers of a racetrack, until they hit a heavy run of pitches.

At other times, the fanners rode their wood sleighs on the trails to woodlots in skeleton, with the sides and bottoms removed, stakes stemming from the bunk holes, the drivers standing spread-foot sideways on two bunks.

There the axes of winter rang in lonely echo. And the cross-cut saws see-sawed in their sidewise bite, with two men kneeling, their arms pumping like the drivers of a locomotive, the saw teeth barely missing their upright shins, the spurting sawdust speckling their gumboots and the snow at their toes.

Then, on moonlit evenings, the blood mares drew the pung and jaunting sleighs, their tails and manes a wisping blur, their swift hooves flipping fragments of snow over the dashboards and peppering the buffalos and ticking of the leather mitts, their shadows bobbing, weaving and poking at the white-capped fence posts sailing past.

The January thaw gave an interesting twist to the scene. The snow sank, and with it torrents of rain and rivers and lakes appeared in low-lying areas, horses plunged and sleighs float-ed. With the freeze, the snow turned to the texture of bread dough, the rivers and lakes to glass-hard sheets of ice that would "pick" from the sharp corks of horseshoes, and the sleighs would slew and side-haul at the horses.

And there were scenes of harshness, too: of horses fighting their way through cold, blasting ground drifts while the driv-ers, their heads ducked into their collars, one-handed the reins and school children huddled under buffalos fighting off a numbing chill.

Winter on Hook Road

CHAPTER 4

There were three major happenings that winter. The first, according to the old timers, was what qualified as an old-fashioned winter. It was not in league with the storm of '26, when they could see only the rooftops of the houses in town and they had to bring in food by toboggan. But by the standards of the day, it was a hair-raiser.

It came just after the January thaw, and we were pretty much confined to base for about a week. Outside, the wind went raving mad and the old house creaked and groaned as if in the throes of a nightmare. Aside from the day's threshing, we only left the house to hack junks of beef off the carcass hanging in the shop, feed and water the stock, milk the farr cow and keep the manure accumulation to some kind of toleration by piling it outside the cow-stable door.

Going to the barn in itself was a venture. When you opened the back door the wind would try to snap it out of your grasp and fight your closing it, then belt you, suck at your breath and lash your eyes with fine snow. You'd lean against the house for a breather and catch glimpses of the barn peak flashing through the white blast.

Then you would have to have to fight your way, sometimes held to a standstill, finally stumbling from the sudden release, into the lee of the barn.

The cold was never far away in the house. The water and milk buckets skimmed heavy with ice. Snow snuffed through the crack under the front door, and through the spaces at the window sashes. The windowpanes were blanked white with thick, furry, fancy frost patterns. The lamp would flicker and smoke from drafts coming from several directions. Some nights we didn't go to bed at all. It was too cold, even with all your clothes on, heated bricks at your feet and a stack of bedclothes supplemented with an overcoat. We huddled around the kitchen stove with our feet on the oven door, listening to the radio, playing twenty questions or listening to The Boss tell his tales of yesterday.

He could do a pretty good job when he got his pipe tucked into his cheek and the muse came into his eyes. He was almost as good as Tom Dougal, and like Tom, he didn't just tell stories, he painted pictures. When he talked about the time he fell asleep driving the stumper at five years old, I saw the small bare feet, tanned and clay-speckled, dangling from the capstan top, the small head nodding at times, the reins beginning to slither through the small hands; saw the heavy plug horse hitched to the arm extending from the capstan top, his tail lazily sweeping at droning flies, a sifter bowl guarding him from nose flies, an empty feed bag hanging on one of his hame's horns. A few yards away, the large stump leaned at a steep angle, its smaller roots running like veins through clinging clods of earth, its larger ones, broken or hoe-cut, creating a ragged fan.

And I saw the men bringing solid, thumping cuts to the roots of a stump, pausing to brush at blackflies, their exposed forearms glistening in the sun; saw the smoke rising from the grey ashes of the lunchtime fire, sweeping lazily over stump holes and clay-spattered brush, grouping and settling around the jumble of stump heads and root fans at the clearing's edge. And I saw my great-grandfather garner the boy in his arms, lay him at the shade of a tree so he could sleep.

I was never at the mud beds, but when The Boss talked about them I came close. I could see the man guiding the horse on the roundabout, pulling at the capstan arm, a cold ground drift sweeping the ice; hear the *queeze* in the twin upright beams of the digger frame as the chain rattled through the pulley centring the crossbeam; see the chain running up from the slush-speckled water until the fork head suddenly appeared with a *splunge* to rise in its swing and halt, hovering over the bobsleigh siding the uprights; see the digger man at the end of the beam pulling the rod on the beams back, and the fork head dropping a glob of sloppy black mud into the sleigh box.

And I felt I was there when The Boss balanced himself in the wood sleigh with the horse frog-leaping, sometimes disappearing in the wild white swirl of a blizzard, heading out for the doctor when my father was born.

He had gotten Joe Mason to take Mabel over to be with

Nanny while he and Tom Dougal fought their way into town. They wore out three horses in the seven-mile trip. They would cover each horse with a buffalo as it played out, and get a fresh one from the nearest farmstead. And I could see the two men in their slow, tormenting journey, beating their arms, stamping their feet, taking turns at the reins and wading out to clear snow from the horse's nostrils; see them urging at the horse's bridle, with the horse down and snow-stuck, then finally standing wind-whipped in the blast, yelling and gesturing, their words muted by the wind. The stories didn't make the wind and cold go away, but they helped make the night go by.

We threshed grain on the third day after the storm set in. The thresher was in a short loft above the barn floor. The engine sat on the barn floor with the belt running up at a fairly steep angle. The thresher resembled some kind of animal with its long jaw, humped back and long, square tail, and when it began to hum its mill, rattle its grain trough, shake straw off its tail with a *wrack-a-wrack-a-wracka*, the loft girders trembled, the barn jiggled and your teeth rattled. All other sounds were drowned out: the thud of the sheaves that Nanny threw down from the loft hitting the table, the pucks of the engine, the swish of the grain stalks The Boss fed into the thresher's mouth after cutting the sheaf bands with a mower-blade tooth on a stick.

I tailed the shaker: hauling back the straw from the rear end with a fork, my eyes slitted against the blowing chaff, my nostrils smudged by blowing black smut. I can't say I ever cared much for tailing the shaker; I never knew anybody that did.

We did some grading then, down in the cellar where it was damp, cold and confined, where time got bogged down amidst the snuff of The Boss clearing his nose with his thumb and forefinger, the cobble of potatoes as he rolled them—picking out the bluenose, seconds, jumbo and rot—and the hiss of the gas lantern hanging from a rafter. The lantern's glow fell on the potatoes and humped the slanting grader, with its slat bottom and board sides, but didn't touch much else. The grader's four thin legs and the bag hanging at its mouth were in semi-darkness; there was blackness at the top of the potato pile, and shadows cupped the few potatoes sheeted by light. In their corner, the weigh scales stood vague, the vertical post and the horizontal arm with the balance bar beneath forming a gloomy F. The pile of bagged potatoes was a black block. When you moved, those big, gloomy shadows would bob around. A slight dust would rise from the rolling potatoes and its choke would mingle with smells of the cellar's brick clay, the lantern's naphtha gas, the rotting potatoes and the septic-smelling pile of new bags by the grader. And it all combined to a boredom you could cut with a knife.

I took care of weighing, sewing and piling the bags and forking them on. I used to see how fast I could sew up a bag: working the long-handled needle and twine through the edges of the bag mouth, looping the ears and tying on the tag. Then I'd try furling the bag off a knee boost onto the pile without knocking it down.

Between bags, I'd take the short, D-handled potato fork, with its multi-tined bowl, and fork on, seeing how fast I could do that without spilling potatoes over the side of the grader or crowding The Boss. I guess you could say I didn't care too much for grading either.

But we couldn't go too far with grading, in case the potatoes sprouted in the bags before we could move them out. Pumping water for the animals and throwing down hay was all we had for heavy work then. Not much to do clear of that but get the time in.

I read what I could find. Me and The Boss played cards until we got sick of it. Then we went at crokinole for a while. We wound up working the jigsaw puzzle Aunt Laura gave us for Christmas. It pictured a Venetian boatman oaring a curled-up gondola past water-cut, autumn-coloured buildings. It took up half the kitchen table. Nanny didn't seem to mind though. Kept knitting and cooking, fooled around with the puzzle once in a while.

Coming on toward the end of the storm, we ran out of salt and molasses and began double-boiling the tea to stretch it out. The Boss ran out of tobacco; tore up whatever butts he could find for cigarettes until there were no more to scrounge and he was out of papers anyway. He took a crack at a dried-out cud of plug, shredded and wrapped in newspaper. We were short of matches, too, and he used a splinter held between his thumb and forefinger to light his horn-like roll. He poked the splinter into the stove and it came out with a heavy flare; it lit things up pretty good, and then there was this flame running toward his face, getting bigger, and he whipped it away and wrung it, it blazing all the more, until he dropped it and stomped it into the floor in a cloud of smoke.

"Anything left for a curtain call?" Nanny said. "Why didn't

you use your pipe?"

"Mind your own business," The Old Man said. He had his eyebrows scorched a bit; there was a brown patch here and there among the grey. He got kind of grouchy then, pretty much kept to solitaire and the radio for the rest of the day. I was getting to the point of missing school; even took a look at my books.

But sometime during the night, the wind relented and, like some kind of animal that failed to devour, skulked away. In the morning, the house was warm again, and quiet. The song of the kettle was not disturbed by house creaks and wind howls; the morning music on the radio was not disturbed by static.

Outside, there was that glistening white in a bright, cold stillness. The pillar of smoke from Tom Dougal's chimney rose straight up. Across the fields, Joe Mason was breaking the road, standing sideways in the wood sleigh, one-handing the reins, his arm extending straight. His horse was labouring in the heavier drifts, sometimes frog-leaping, its head wagging with the effort, its breath mingling with the steam rising from its back. And when he reached the wind-swept bowl in our yard, he had to leap down, for the wind-blown snow had formed a cliff.

The Old Man sang out to Joe from the horse stable: "Enough snow down for you, Joe?"

"A little more and we'll be climbing mountains, or digging tunnels," Joe said without stopping.

Our road allotment ran out our south lane and west to the end of Jar, where the Calders lived, just beside the short woods road leading to Albert Leland's warehouse. People from the other district came through there in the winter.

When I finally got going, after poking for the sleigh through two feet of snow and shovelling out, I pretty well had to break the road all over again. The snow was piled up at our gateway so bad, I had to cut our fence fifty yards from our gateway, work my way around the heaviest part and cut the Calder fence to get onto the road.

It was quite a job getting the manure out—all the weaving and meandering around drifts—and there was just one patch of the snake-like pile visible. I had to take a guess and fork off where I thought the end would be. It took me all day.

On the way to the village next day, where the sleigh road ran along a ways with the railroad, you could see the blocks of snow flying from shovel heads, coming seemingly out of the white in their quick shoot and drop from the railroad cutting. The pass of a locomotive was identified only by its slanting smoke billow, rising to mingle with the drifting snow in its cold ground sweep. At the crossing, you could see the ledges tiering the solid white walls of the cutting, where men bent, rammed their shovels, straightened and hurled the snow to the next level, their shovels sweeps followed by white, powdery swirls, adding to the coldness of the scene.

The storm left, but the cold hung around. That hit home the hardest when we got back to school. The stove was hot enough. Its heat waves rose up the vertical pipe and waggled a cobweb hanging just past the elbow on the wire-hung vertical pipe running to the safe in the wall. Those near it sat in their sweaters with sweaty hands. But those in far comers sat leg-locked, breathing out white puffs, in their coats, overshoes and mitts.

Going to the outhouse was an experience. Except for a crust of snuffed-in snow by the door and the light shaft slanting from the small, square open window, it was dark, for starters. Working off your pants and getting your underwear flap properly gapped in the cold exposure wasn't too pleasant either. I'm not even going to mention too much about having to touch down on the hole, except that the elements and individual endurance definitely played a part in the sitting time. They played an even bigger part in the hand wash at the icicle-bearded pump in the yard with a tin cup hanging from its nose.

The cold snap hung on until well after Tom Dougal's death: the second major happening that winter.

Tom's property frontage was on both sides of the road, running from our line and Joe Mason's down to the brook. His farmstead buildings were about fifty yards in from the road on Joe's side. He and his wife, Ethel, lived with young Tom, his son, and his wife, Ruth. The rest of his children, three boys and three girls, were all married and living away. Young Tom had pretty much taken over the farm. He was a dead ringer for his dad: stout and slightly paunchy, with a block head, bushy hair and eyebrows, and a kindly slant to his eyes.

Old Tom was the best I ever heard at telling a story or a yarn. I'll never forget the evening Wally Mason and I had dropped in a couple of years back and Tom was in the right mood. When Ethel let us in, he was in the middle of lighting his crooked stem pipe with a lighted splinter; his eyes, peering from under his bushy eyebrows, growing bigger with each draw on the pipe bit, each cheek-denting pull hauling a ragged flame into the packed bowl, until a huge puff of smoke came and wiped it out.

The cold of a crisp winter evening clung to our clothes and our numb fingers. We found a seat by the stove, purring its warmth in tune with the *tick-tock* of the grandfather clock on the wall. We mentioned the cold.

Tom let out another belch of smoke that hung wave-like in the air, a bushy eyebrow cocked and he was off:

"Cold! Why, you don't know what cold is. Now, out in western Canada, back before the big war, it got so cold one night I set a kettle of boiling water outside on the doorstep, and it froze so fast I had hot ice. Yeh, two hundred and ten below zero. Went to kick the cat out the door and froze me foot, just like that, quick as a wink. They dang near had to cut off me big toe. It's never been right since. Yeh, why I seen a rabbit take a hop and freeze right in mid-air and he hung right there until the first cheenook wind came along and thawed things out."

"What's a cheenook wind?" I said.

There was silence for a moment. Tom took a few quick drags on his pipe, his stubby fingers pressing into the pipe bowl between puffs. The bushy eyebrow cocked again and Tom's voice took on a mysterious monotone.

"Nothing can thaw things out like a cheenook wind. One winter there was thirty feet of snow, flat level, and it colder than a witch's breath. I mind I was coming from town one day in a two-horse bobsleigh. All of a sudden, this warm wind began to blow out of nowhere. Well, sir, it melted the snow so fast, only the front bobs were on snow. The hind ones were in mud and not twenty yards behind, there was me dog choking in dust. That's the winter we ran out of hay and had to put sunglasses on the cows so they'd eat the snow. Yeh."

Through the whole story, Tom's face, smoke hanging at his bushy eyebrows, was completely sober, completely serious. You could swear he believed every word.

Old Tom had got religion the past year. Some said it was because he'd been sick. He'd quit smoking and chewing and taking a nip at Christmas and special occasions. He never did swear; always a good living man, great neighbour.

We got word at the general store on a Saturday afternoon. I was standing by the post office section at the front end of the long counter, looking out through the high, wide window by the glass-panelled door.

A dusty beam of late afternoon sun, slanting through the window on the west side, was cutting at the shoulder of the pasteboard cigarette girl sitting in the far side of the window space. Its sharp glow was silhouetting the molasses lassie in the near side. Partly obscured by the signs, the faces of two tethered horses hung, their large eyes shadowed by the leather flaps of their blind bridles, white puffs curling from their nostrils, steam streaks weaving from their buffalo-covered backs. Now and then, through the spaces of unobstructed view, beyond the horses, glimpses of brightly clad children flashed, the jugs of their peak caps flopping wing-like at the sides of their small reddened faces, their mittened hands arcing, flinging tightly packed snowballs. I was waiting for The

Boss while Frank Brown, the storekeeper—perched on a ladder, picking goods from the shelves, which tiered almost from the floor to the ceiling on the side wall—was working our grocery list. At the stove, at the back of the long alley-like room, John Avery and Pete White were bantering with the one known as Trader Sam. Sam had recently jig-skipped in around the door, his feet hitting the floor with the door's slam, his arms held out in stage fashion. There were chuckles as the short man ambled to the stove with his bloated overall pant legs stuffed into his short rubber boots and his pulled-up coat collars joining with his cap peak to frame a fat face with a pointed nose, quick eyes and a quick lip.

"That's right, boys," Sam was saying. "I'd trade anything but me wife."

"You'd trade her, too, if she had the heaves," John Avery said.

"Now you know me better than that, John," Sam said. "I never traded a heaving horse in me life."

"I never knew you to trade a horse that didn't have the heaves," Pete White said.

"Well, Pete, right now I got the best horse I ever had or seen and he ain't got no heaves."

"Has he got any speed?" Pete said.

"Now you see him and now you don't, and he can haul, too. I had him hauling logs the other day and one of the sleigh bunks caught on a stump and didn't he break both traces and it never took a fizz out of him. Now I wouldn't lie to you. He just whipped out of there like nobody's business."

"I'm not surprised, with the kind of harness you got," John said.

"Now, John, there ain't nothing wrong with my…"

The bell over the door jangled and Joe Mason stepped in. The soberness of his demeanour grabbed our attention.

"Old Tom's gone, boys," Joe said. "Passed away about an hour ago."

The stark reality hitting home seemed to freeze the room in that greyness.

Old Tom had been especially bad for the past few weeks. When I'd been forking off a sleigh-load of manure in the field earlier that morning, I'd noticed the doctor's rig at Tom's door. The Old Man and I had been planning to drop in on the way home.

"Young Tom asked me to look after getting the grave dug," Joe Mason said. "I got Jim and Alban and Charlie. Dan will probably come."

"I'll be there," The Boss said.

"You come up short, let me know," Sam said.

"The same here," John Avery said.

Joe nodded. "I guess we'll get at her early tomorrow. We're going to need picks and crowbars."

They had to pick and crowbar their way through four and a half feet of ground, frozen solid, and a foot and a half of brick clay to get the grave dug.

Old Tom had passed away quietly. After the work of the undertaker, he lay with a peaceful look in the cushioned coffin in the Dougal living room, amidst the sickly sweet smell that surrounds all biers. Friends and relatives came softly into the room to shake hands with the family and take their last look by the coffin. Most didn't wait around for long, but long enough for respect; when they spoke, it was in hushed tones.

It was cold in the church the day of the funeral. The wood stove there could not force the chill from much farther than the nearest pews. The nail heads in the walls, void of insulation, were white with frost.

At the singing of "Shall We Gather at the River," to the wheeze and drone of a pump organ, the minister actually dropped his hymnal to blow on his fingers.

Ethel, wrinkled and grey, stood with a peaceful acceptance that showed mostly on her face, which was speckled by a black veil. Her children, now solid men and prim ladies, held the hands of their children. The peaceful look of acceptance rested on their faces as well. At the close of the hymn, the minister could not resist hiding his hands behind the pulpit to rub them warm. Then, opening his worn Bible, he read:

"For God so loved the world, that He gave His only begotten Son, that whosoever believeth in him should not perish, but hath everlasting life."

The preacher's words, somewhat stiffened by the chill in his lips, rose and fell in resounding echo. When the reading was through, he paused for a moment to study the people sitting rigid in their pews. Then he began his eulogy:

"We all know what kind of man Tom was: honest, upright, charitable and hard-working. But he was more than that. He was a man who sought after the things of God.

"I visited Tom a few days before his death. I can still see him sitting in his old rocker, talking of life, its joys, labour and brevity, and what life really is. And this is pretty much what he had to say:

'I worked hard, long as I can remember. I worked hard. I made this property what is with what God gave me. I cleared the land in the back field with a horse and stumper and I hauled mud in the cold of winter and spread it on the land with a shovel. I work in the fields from sun up to sun down. I took my rest on the Sabbath, and took my family to church. I earned what I got by the sweat of my brow and I did my best to teach my children what was right, and to have respect for their fellow man.

'Now my time grows short. That's how life is and I will soon meet my maker; I will meet him prepared. But it wasn't the things I mentioned that prepared me. It wasn't the way I worked, or what I taught, or how honest I was. For with all the right things I did, there was still sin.

'But not long ago, I discovered that Jesus died for sinners, me included, and I sought forgiveness from God through him. For it was his death on the cross that saves, not anything I could do.

'That's the secret to life: being ready to meet your maker. This land, my family, and the health to enjoy both are marvellous gifts; they're from the hand of God. But the greatest gift of all is eternal life in heaven, for nothing else lasts.'"

There was no way they could get the road open for the motor hearse; they had to use the sleigh hearse hauled by a jet-black horse, with its long windows and curtains and its coach-like seat on the front, where the undertaker and his assistant sat.

At the grave, the icy wind blew; its mourn seemed in tune with the chill of death. The ground drift of powdery snow swept over the green blanket on the mound of clay, blowing in our faces and flapping our coat tails as we sang "Abide With Me" through chattering teeth. The wind blew the clay as it fell from the minister's hand, scattering it across the coffin at "ashes to ashes and dust to dust." A body was commended to the earth and a soul was commended to God.

The Boss took it harder than he let on. He and Old Tom had been through a lot together. They had stuck by each other through a lot of cold, hard times, the kind of times that knit men's souls together. You couldn't call The Boss religious. He had his own reverential fear of God; he'd listen to the hellfire preaching on the radio on Sunday mornings, badger me to go to church, but he was no churchgoer himself. But when Old Tom changed to religion, and neighbourly attitudes changed, too, there was no difference as far as The Old Man was concerned. They had their arguments about the Bible and whatnot, but The Boss respected Old Tom's beliefs; and I guess if he could tell it, since Old Tom took up religion, he'd been getting soft toward it himself.

On the way home from the funeral, when we turned from the trail angling down across John Cobly's field and headed for the bridge at the creek, one heavy tear streaked down The Old Man's face and froze at his jaw. And there was a reverential sadness in his voice that spoke of memories, nostalgia and loss when he said, "God never made a better man than Tom Dougal."

The hockey team won the cup that year for the first and last time: the third major happening that winter. Formed within the district and surrounding areas, their individual skills nurtured on frozen ponds, the team always gave a solid effort. But they'd had nothing of the spectacular to give them the edge until Charlie Wallace began to mature, and that winter he peaked.

Due to the inevitable two-week flu, being caught up in my guitar and practising now and then with Wally Mason, I missed most of the games up to the cup-winner. If King hadn't thrown a shoe, and The Boss hadn't sent me down to the Wallaces' to get him shod, I probably would have missed it, too.

I knew I was going at a good time when, after skirting the spring hole in Dan Coulter's field and topping the sharp rise at the end of the gap through his woods, I could see the grey-blue smoke rising from the mill toward an overcast sky.

If Alf had been working at some weird gadget, I probably would have had to wait awhile before he got to me. Turned out he was shaping a brace for a plow, just finishing off when I got there. He paused in mid-swing, looking at me when he spoke, his large eyes staring white through the sweat-streaked soot and smoke on his face, his brow furrowed as if to keep the eyes open, the veins on his hands bulging worm-like through sweaty grit.

"Bring him in," he said, reaching for the square, basket-like tool box that was hanging on a peg on the wall. I unhitched King and led him into the small, low-ceilinged shop, his hooves clomping on the worn and pitted floor planks.

For Alf's size, short and slightly humped, with oil-can shoulders and not a lot of meat on him, he did a credible job at blacksmithing. I held King's halter and watched as Alf butted rear ends with the horse and tucked his right hind foot between his thighs. Working deft and quick, he cleared the frog with the curved knife, trimmed the hoof with the tong-like cutters, rasped it all smooth and lay on a blank shoe to gauge.

"How long have you been blacksmithing?" I said.

Alf dropped the horse's foot and, with a pair of tongs, stuffed the shoe into the glowing crack in the crusted coals in the forage, then pumped the forage handle. The hot light blazed; blue-grey smoke puffed from the coals and billowed up through the square hole in the roof peak; ragged blue-grey waves hovered over the flop-mouthed bag of coal hunched by the disorderly pile of scrap metal; blue-grey fingers pointed at the square rods of cork steel reclining against the rough, open-studded wall and the row of blank horseshoes hooked on a wire between two studs; a blue-grey halo hung over the horned anvil sitting squat on its block.

"Shoed my first horse when I was fifteen," he finally said. "Picked it up watching Gabe Grant in town. Got Gabe to let me try a horse. Got kicked against the wall right off, but Gabe let me at it, teaching me as I went along."

Alf had taken the shoe from the forge and was talking between heavy hammer blows at the anvil as he bent the shoe tips into sharpened ells. He stuffed the shoe back into the coals, round end first, and with a length of cork steel.

"Persuaded the old man to buy me the gear from the cata-logue." Alf concentrated on cutting off a wedge of white hot cork on the hardy, hammering it into the shoe round with a loud pop, then hammering it sharp, before he spoke again.

"Yep, shoed a lot of horses since then; only thing I like better than inventing." He rammed the shoe into a cask of water and was engulfed in a cloud of acrid steam that mingled with the smells of burnt coal, hot metal, smoke and horse.

With the horse's foot tucked between his thighs again, Alf nailed on the shoe, driving the flat-headed nails through the hoof with whacks of the toy-like hammer and nubbing them. He finished with a final rasp dressing, with the foot resting on a tripod-like rest.

"That'll do him," Alf said. He swiped a dipper of water from a bucket and drank heavily with twin drools.

I held a two-dollar bill out to him while he took a fig of twist from his pocket and bit off a junk. He worked the cud for a bit, studying the floor. Finally, he spat a squirt of tobacco juice, eyed me sideways and said, "Tell you what. I'm thinking of building a wood sleigh. You keep the money and tell Harv to keep an eye out for a decent maple stick with the right curve for runners—he should have something in his woods—and we'll call her square."

I mentioned to him that I had a message for George from The Boss concerning a meeting for the school trustees. "You better go down to the cellar and tell him yourself in case I forget," Alf said. "Him and Charlie are grading. Just leave the horse here until you get back."

In the cellar, George stood big, bulky and hunched over the grader. He had a glint of disdain in his pig-like eyes, and his big mouth and round, fleshy face were contorted into a cringe.

"How's she going, Jake?" Charlie said from behind the grader.

"You're driving 'er," I said.

"Were driving 'er," Charlie said. "Cooking with gas."

In stature, Charlie was somewhere between Alf and George. His face, except for George's eyes, pretty much belonged to his mother, Hilda: slightly lean with a heavy brow and a mischievous hawkishness.

"Yes, and if he don't stop stinking, he'll be working by himself," George growled. "Stinking mortal."

Charlie halted and rested the half-empty fork against the potatoes piled on the grader, his eyes going into a piggish stare.

George went rigid, his eyes peering sharply at me, the disdain on his face growing into a red flush. "Didn't I tell you, didn't I tell you?" he said. "Stinking mortal. No manners. He'll go in a church, at a funeral, in a restaurant, at the table; he don't care. He just cocks that big rump of his and lets 'er go. And stink! He'd gas a horse! Ah, that's enough. Grade the dog-gone potatoes yourself." George stomped up the stone cellar steps and out, dropping the cellar hatch with a whump.

Charlie's tongue flopped out in a giddy laugh.

"You're an awful man, Charlie," I said when I got over my laugh seizure.

"I'm an awful man," Charlie said.

"You must have been eating beans."

"I don't need beans."

When we finally sobered up, I asked about the hockey play-offs, and the big game Saturday night.

"We're going to win 'er," Charlie said. "Be there. They'll be hanging from the rafters. They're laying on a truck from the village."

"I'm just getting over the flu," I said.

"Never mind that. You don't want to miss it, flu or no flu. We're going to bring home the bacon."

"I got a message for George, so I better get a move on."

"Tell him he can come back down to work, but he'll have to stop stinking," Charlie said with a wry smirk.

George had King hitched to the sleigh and was waiting, holding him by the bridle. He glanced around the horse at me as I gave him the message.

"Safe to go down now?" he said when I finished. "Fog cleared away?"

"I think so," I said.

"Stinking mortal."

It was calm that Saturday evening as I walked into the village, with just a light winter freshness. It was late in March and there were patches of bare ground showing and the snow was beginning to honeycomb. As I came into the village, with the gloom of darkness setting in, I could hear Fred James's three-ton truck chugging in idle. Stubby, round-faced Willy Walters, the driver, took my quarter by the tail end. Hands reached down from the block of darkness —framed by the truck's racks and overlaid tarp roof—and I was hauled over by the arms. I worked my way among jammed-in bodies for a place to stand.

"Are we all here? Are all the chickens in?" Willy hollered above the truck's rumble.

A voice came out of the darkness, sounding dry and strange: "Yeah, we're all here. Put 'er in the big cog and drive 'er."

Presently, the truck jerked forward and rocked its way along, bumping, jostling and crowd-jamming us at the turns, its motor song rising to the gear changes, purring at high, breaking abruptly at the upgrade, mingling with the conversations, murmurs and yelps. Now and then a cut rhyme or a song parody was belted out, followed by laughter. There was a gale of howls as our feet left the floor to return with a teeth-jolting thump when the truck bumped off the pavement and headed down a muddy shortcut. Suddenly, the truck's momentum began to grow heavy and the pauses and jerks of gear changes worked toward bull low.

A laboured thrust of the truck dragged to a halt; a backward jolt went nowhere; the motor sounded like an angry, captive bee, buzzing slightly above the whirr of wheels spinning in mud.

The motor was cut and we stood in a silence made eerie by the sudden absence of truck sounds. Those of us at the front began prying up an overlap in the tarp for a look. In the weak bask of the truck's lights, I could see a patch of deep mud scarred by snaking wheel ruts where vehicles had fought their way through. Willy Walters, having left the cab, was wading out into the slop, slowly looking around, his shadow poking here and there as if trying to find a way out.

"You want us to get off and try pushing?" Al Avery called through the tarp opening.

"I guess we could try that," Willy said. We piled off over the back and gave it a shot, but we didn't gain much, if any. With the truck's sides anywhere from chest level to over the head, depending on the individual, and our feet lodging in mud, the best most of us could do was get mud-splattered from the spin of the wheels. More than a few were plastered before Willy gave up and went for a tractor.

We stood waiting by the road in total darkness. Our ardour had turned to a glum silence. Then fat Bob Swain sung out, his voice sounding strange in the night. "Cheer up folks, better days ahead. If we don't get a tractor we'll hijack the next mule train."

Suddenly a chorus of "Irene, Goodnight" broke out. Then we heard the rumble of a distant tractor and twin lights swept onto the road and headed our way, jigging and weaving and growing ever broader.

In time, the lights swept the front of the truck, and the tractor slew into a U-turn and came to a halt. A chain began to rattle and clank and the tractor's tail light began to play peekaboo with Willy's body as he got the draw bar chained up with the truck's bumper. It took a bit of slewing around and chain-jerking in different directions—with the tractor churning, roaring and fish-tailing, and the truck pretty much the same—but they got her out and we got on board again.

"I guess we won't need the mule train," Fat Bob said.

"Is everybody happy?" Willy roared.

"Yeah, we're all happy! Put 'er in the big cog and drive her," came the voice in the dark.

It took a while to find our feet when we piled off the truck, after jostling in the dark for balance. Some of us were still wobbly as we made our way past the few other cars and trucks parked with their snouts poking from the shade of the rink. The rink was old, with ragged steel siding curling at the seams. Over the battered board entrance door, a naked bulb threw a shallow glow from its curved pipe fixture. Inside the entranceway, a cold draft seeped through the cracks in the heaving board floor. A cold blast hit me at the ticket window when I handed in my quarter and got my halved ticket. As I passed into the tunnel-like walkway at the front of the ice surface, I glanced through the chicken wire and saw rink attendants slide-stepping on the ice, pushing locked scrapers, herding a wave of water into the snow hole in a square corner of the boards.

All the players were on the ice. Our team was on the near blue line waiting for the attendants to finish so they could take their shots at the goalie. Only their sweaters were the same; their pants and socks varied in colour and they had a lot of holes exposing equipment parts. There were usually gaps between the socks and pants, exposing bare flesh or grimy underwear. Some players looked like they were moulting.

I paused to watch, somewhat in awe, as my heroes began to glide in on the crouching goalie to take their shots. On scuffed skates, with lengths of felt under the laces for tightness and flopping over the toes for protection, they swooped in like hunched vultures. I noted every swerve, sweep and twitch—things I would try to copy on a frozen pond.

Eventually I made my way to the men's dressing room door, which was battered and scarred by carelessly slung skates and swung with a creak against its worm-like return spring. As I sidled my way inside, jostled by bodies, I could feel beneath my feet the tin patches nailed over the rough board floor where skate blades had worn through. The smells of stale cigarette smoke, burning coal, frost, disinfectant and urine hit me in a rush and when I took my turn at the tin bowl nailed against the back wall, I got a whiff of black rum and caught a glimpse of a quick swig and a bottle being shoved inside an overcoat.

When I finally got all the buttons fastened on the two pairs of pants, with the binding of my overcoat and the hindrance of its skirts, I paused to catch some heat at the pot-bellied stove. But not for long; there was a sudden roar from the crowd and I knew I was missing something.

Outside the dressing room, the crowd was everywhere: packed standing along the boards, on the boards holding on to chicken wire or rafter supports. The only vacant space I could see was the square top of a goal judge box. I had to squeeze and shove my way through bodies and claw up chicken wire to get there.

I was just in time to see a big, lumbering player with a skullcap bearing in on the one known as the Shorthorn Bull. Skullcap swerved to go by. Suddenly, there was a flash of quick-stepping skates and a solid rear-end shot out and Skullcap went feet up and nose down as Shorthorn nailed him.

Voices rose above the crowd's roar: "Boo! Boo! You'll never get by him that way, you dumb ape." "Dirty Shorthorn Bull, go back to your stall." "Cigarettes, cigarettes, butts, butts, butts. Referee, referee, nuts, nuts, nuts."

And it was up and down the ice in a flurry of pumping legs and chopping skates: circling, weaving, twisting, turning, dipsy-doodling; desperately coming close and getting flattened at the last instant; making the crowd "ooh" and "ahh"; ragging the puck and winging it; elbowing, kneeing, whatever got the job done; arguing with the ref; in exasperation, belting the penalty box door in angry entrance. They played the game as if for the Stanley Cup.

Suddenly the referee was racing to a corner where Skullcap and the Shorthorn had locked horns. There was a tense moment of gripping strength with lip-curled snarls before they hit the ice in a sprawling flop. Skullcap wound up on top, but on the way down Shorthorn got the neck hold on him. With arms that could muscle a hundred-pound bag of potatoes like a steel vice at his neck, Skullcap soon resigned, wagging his head and working his neck, as he made his way to the sin bin. The roar of the crowd was deafening. Insults were hurled. At the sideboards, the crowd swayed and broke and fists flashed.

Play resumed, but soon a cowbell *clunk-a-lunked* and the sweating, puffing players filed toward their dressing rooms to chew at oranges, mutter at the missed shot, the dirty knee and the worthless ref.

I had a nickel and I was tempted to go for a bag of chips at the canteen. I could see the top of its door above the bobbing heads of the lined-up crowd, jamming for their turn to buy. Suddenly the struggle to the confined room, halved by a counter, smelling heavily of steamed hot dogs, where attendants worked furiously in gloomy light, seemed like a lot for a nickel bag of chips. A fellow could get stomped on. Besides, I could lose my place.

Instead, I sat and watched the ice cleaners skate and push slush with canted scrapers in rhythm with "Sweet Rosie O'Grady" coming scratchily from I'm not sure where. The lighting was shallow now, for half the shaded lights, dangling by their cords in their rows from the rafters, had been cut. Faded shadows followed the workers as they went frankly about their work, their skates and lower shins for the most part hidden in a woolly mist rising from the ice. One enterprising individual was skating around them, catching money in a stocking cap to cater from the concession stand.

Before long, the cowbell *clunk-a-lunked* again and the game went on with the gliding, pumping and grinding. The second period passed, the third carried on. Soon, all too soon, the round-faced clock hanging on the back wall in the penalty box said five minutes left. At the end of the rink, the slotted numbers said 4–4. My heroes were working the puck at the other end and I was with them. My shoulder hitched at the deke; my arms went up as the red light above the goal judge glowed through the mill of players and fog.

There was pause in the action, both sides checking strategies with anxious head nods as they got set for the faceoff. The puck was dropped. There was the quick chop of a stick in a pass and once more Skullcap was bearing down on Shorthorn with the puck. Shorthorn was backing, confident; he made his skate-chopping veer. At the last moment, Skullcap shifted and Shorthorn was faked out. Skullcap bore in alone on the goalie, almost in a gallop, with fire in his eyes. The goalie poised in his crouch, his eyes concentrated. The roar of the crowd was like a wall. Suddenly the puck winged and ticked off the inside corner of the square net. The goalie took a fearful backward glance, then swept out the puck with downcast eyes. A call rose above the uproar: "Boo! Boo!

Shorthorn Bull, you didn't do so hot that time. Go home and fork manure." It didn't seem reasonable to get scored on at time like this.

That's when Charlie broke loose, seizing the puck after the draw, and with long, smooth strides, his stick shifting like a magic wand, he darted, swaggered and quick-turned like a frolicking colt. They'd managed to smother him all night, but now he was in control. They'd swipe at the puck, but he'd sweep it away like it was glued to his stick. They'd lunge at him with checks, but he'd be gone, leaving them to thump the boards or take a falling slide through the slush and water.

The goalie at the other end, watching the helplessness before him, had a tense, fearful expression on his face. He made his move at Charlie's deke, but he, too, took a slide through the slush and water. As the puck sailed into the net it was game over, even before the cowbell clunked its last.

The jubilation rode on us like a crown and our steps were light as we made our way back to the truck and climbed aboard.

"Are all the chickens in?" Willy Walters roared.

"Anybody not here speak up," came the voice from the dark.

"Yeah, we're all here. Put 'er in the big cog and drive her."

"Who won the game?" Willy roared.

A mixed chorus roared back: "The Royals!"

Prelude to
Spring on Hook Road

When the snow began to honeycomb, sink under the hot sun and chill to an ice crust in the night; when the poles in the loft bed began to appear amidst patches of grey, dry hay that came up with the fork tines in flakes; when the times of birth came in the cow stalls and a farmer would spend hours with his feet braced against a group edge, straining on a rope looped around yellow hooves pointing from a swollen vulva, holding with the mother's heaves until the limp body, wet with slime, slithered into the world to eventually wobble on stick legs, then butt and *sphirp* in a bucket of curdled milk; when the woodpile was low to the ground, then those along Hook Road knew that soon, what snow the sun didn't dissolve, heavy rains would, and in their patches of dirty-brown and grey, the fields would begin to appear once more, with only traces of the packed winter road remaining, now dirty-grey and with yellow stains where the horse buns lay. Soon Hook Road itself would reappear and the muck-slopping would begin.

They junked up what was left of their winter meat then, before it thawed too much, and what meat didn't go to cold storage was bone-stripped, stuffed into cans, salted, lid-sealed and placed in steaming double boilers until the lids popped.

The bones, streaking white through meat remnants, were boiled, too, until they were stripped bare and the meat in the pots had congealed into that waxy crust over a conglomeration of stringy meat and jelly called potted meat.

The sluggishness came on then, and it was good to laze after a quiet suppertime with the door open and a sun-warmed breeze wafting in the choke of drying mud and listen to the countrified music of the suppertime radio show. The sulphur and molasses, cherry-bark steep and whatever came on then, as a remedy for the laze, or the want of a bad taste.

The last of the potatoes in the cellars, bearded now with sprouts, were moved out then, the clay buildup shovelled out. Seed potatoes were piled in bags against walls of barn floors and sheds for the set cutters. And they would huddle in mixed gender around washtubs of potatoes, sitting on backless chairs, crates and milking stools, in patched overalls, tattered coats with nails for buttons, peaked caps and wedging bandanas. And their banter would mingle with the *schlick, schlick* of keen knives, slicing potatoes between black-crusted thumbs and forefingers, and the plops of sets falling into baskets. In dusty granaries, hump-backed fanners were cranked and grain and hayseed were run through and bagged for seeding.

In the meantime, the spring calves, seeing outside for the first time, found their legs and ran bucking, kicking and crashing fences in the pastures.

Then the fields of furrows, flattened by winter snows and spring rains, bleached and dried chalky by the sun and wind, were grudgingly torn by the mats of spring-tooth harrows; with the drivers choking in dust, hauled by the reins in their grasp, their steps falling halting and rigid from the pace.

In keeping with the scenes of spring, bags of fertilizer, lime and sets would appear in their piles on headlands.

The high-wheeled seeders ran in their cross-field weave then, the spouts along their lengthwise boxes shooting down oats and hayseed, the short links of their cover chains jangling.

Then the potato planters would appear, hunched and sneak-stepping like aged cronies, struggling for balance in fertilized grooves, dropping sets at their toes for spacing, their potato sack set pouches hanging heavy on their shoulders. While in their midst, the scant horse hillers with their twin toed-in discs scuffled up rows of hills.

As a final sweeping-away of a dreary winter, the farmers of Hook Road approached their ragged rows of manure with their snow and ice troves, fork-loaded the rotting dung onto wagons and fork-flung it to the sod.

Spring on Hook Road

CHAPTER 5

To the sweet strains of Jim Mackie's fiddle, the thump-*thumpa-thump-thumpa-thump* of his feet, the backing strum of Alban Gallant's guitar, the dancers swept head-high and proud in their majestic swirl—the dainty feet of the ladies skipping light, the heavier feet of the men quick-stepping and hammering the floor. They wove through the grand chain, pranced through the promenade, rocked and whirled together in the swing with now and then a "yuh" and a "tamarack her down."

After having to deal with a harsh winter, then being literally booted into the hectic drudgery of spring, a tyme was just the thing to shake things loose. And I would have to say the tyme they had for Joanie and Charlie did a bang-up job. The whole affair—though it didn't end that way—started out as the major happening that spring. Agnes Cobly brought it to mind when she came collecting just after the crops were in.

Agnes was a good match for John, especially physically: freckle-faced, about the same stubbiness. Her most outstanding feature was her protruding lower lip, which protruded even more after her short speech phrases: "How are youse this evening? Collecting for Joanie and Charlie's wedding. Nice young couple, good for the community. We thought a chest of drawers would be nice. Yep, a dollar would be just fine. Better keep on the go. Don't forget to come up for a game of auction."

The wedding came off pretty much the same as weddings usually go. Charlie had a few belts in him by the time he got to the altar. When the minister asked him if he would take Joanie to be his wife he said, "I'll take her," then he tried to put the ring on Joanie's little finger. There was the usual snuffle around that time of course. After the marriage ceremony, two of the Wallace cousins got into a wagon race on the way from the church to the mill. They both hit the gateway at the same time and a wheel got smashed against a post. The usual sort of thing that makes the occasion memorable.

Alf and George compromised and they held the reception in the mill and the dance in the house parlour. George decided if they tamaracked-her-down on the mill floor, the roof might tamarack-her-down itself. Since he was the father of the groom and Alf was the father of nothing but inventions that never worked anyway, he was entitled to the last say.

Charlie's uncle on his mother's side was the emcee. He was a stout man with a perpetually red face, which blended in well since most of the male faces had a royal flush. He had a bit of a lisp and the more slugs he took from the punch in his glass—replenished from under the table by a nephew with hair over his eyes and a thick-lipped smirk—the more it grew. The lisp became more of a confused slur when the time came to toast the bride. "Now Ahlbhert Wallache will lead us in thishing-ah-tashing-ah-toashting the bird-ah-bhride."

A few minutes after Charlie's speech, a two-minute job that ended with, "I hope you all came to dance cause we're going to drive 'er," something beneath the rough board floor punked and the folding table with the wedding cake shook and the tablecloth flapped and George mentioned that it would be nice to have the cake cutting and all the rest out in the yard in the sunshine. Nobody had to be persuaded.

Charlie drove 'er at the dance that evening, no doubt about that. He said he was going to dance with every single woman there as a parting shot and he pretty well did. Between one of the sets, someone called for him to "give us a step" and right off, to shouts of "drive her" and "tamarack her down," Charlie was prancing to the centre of the floor with mischief in his eyes, mock anger on his face and his neck bowed like a proud horse. Then, hoisting his pant legs in a curtsy in time with the sudden belt of music from Jim and Alban, he toed the floor like he was testing water. Then, like a sudden summer rain, his scuffed shoes drummed, belted, crossed over, quick-stepped and hammered the floor. Then he broke loose. Parting the crowd as he went, he danced his way into the kitchen, where he jumped, clicked his heels, landed on a chair and danced there. Another jump with a heel click and he was dancing on the stove. Then he was on the floor again, dancing his way back into the parlour.

Charlie's act opened the way for what might be called "participation time." Alf took a chair in a conspicuous corner below the mantle where the Aladdin lamp glowed. In a flourish, with a lick of his tongue, he pulled loose his green tie, unbuttoned his shirt, placed both feet flat on the floor and conducted the proceedings. "We'll have theGallants now," Alf said.

And they danced and sang. "Now, George. 'Molly Dee'. Come on." George stood in a far corner with his head canted, pursing his lips.

"Well, I'm not much of a singer," George said.

"Stop putting on the dog, George, and sing," Alf said.

"Come on, George," John Cobly said.

"Show us your stuff," Joe Mason said.

"Well, I don't know all the words," George said. "But..." George steepened his head cant, hitched his shoulders and began in a low foghorn bellow: "Oh, Molly Dee. Oh, please don't cry. Cause I must say goodbye. I'm going to sail, so please don't wail. I've joined the Navy and it won't be gravy. I'm leaving soon as the wind blows high. Oh, blow ye winds and blow them high, the skipper's name is William Nye. Now please don't cry, my Molly Dee..."

"Ah, that's enough, George," Alf said, "if that's the best you can do."

George shot a mean glance at Alf. "Well, I told you I didn't know all the words, big mouth."

"You don't know none of the words. Where's Dan? Come on, Dan, give us a poem."

"Where's Dan?" Charlie said.

"Here, he's coming," John Cobly said.

Dan Coulter, with his tie hanging out and his sleepy eyes peering past a long nose in a thin face, made his way through the gathering to stand hunched and bent-kneed beside Alf. Alf gave no further introduction, other than to throw back his head and hold out a flat hand as an offering. Dan passed his hand over his brow, swiping away a fall of grey hair. Then, directing his gaze at a ceiling corner and holding his hand out palm up in stage fashion, he flapped his oversized lips a few times and began:

> In Carpet Town, there lives a man,
>> by the name of Mr. Jones;
> And t'would take a banker's ledger
>> to list the things he owns.
> He owns the restaurant there, you know,
>> though it's not in his name;
> The ice cream parlour, and the grocery store
>> are underscored the same.
> The hardware store, the bank,
>> the store for shoes and boots;
> He even owns the bootlegging joint,
>> and the house of ill repute.
> I got to know about the gains
>> of this famous Mr. Jones,

When things got slack, a few years back
and I hit him up for a loan.
Then the cows all died, the crops all failed,
so the mortgage just kept growing;
'Til all I had, including me,
belonged to Mr. Jones.
I could go on about it all,
but to minimize my groans,
There was scant few places where I didn't owe
this famous Mr. Jones.
Just the funeral parlour, and oh,
to keep things fair and true;
There is the insurance company,
oh yes, he owns that, too.
About a week or so ago,
I dropped in on old Doc Reeves,
With his scope at me chest, he said in jest,
"Sounds like you got the heaves."
But he really didn't joke at all,
when he said with a kindly face:
"You better get things nailed down, my friend;
you're about to leave the race."
"If I give you an extra fin," I said,
"could you set things up a bit?"

"This man's in good health," he solemnly wrote,
and signed his name to the chit.
Then I ambled down to Jones's bank
for one last goodly loan;
Ere I left the bank I kindly thanked
and shook hands with Mr. Jones.
Then I ambled to the insurance place
like I was on a spree,
And took me out an all-inclusive
insurance policy.
Now me mortgage gets paid, me debts all stayed,
me wife won't have to cry.
They'll bury me in a Jones-built box;
all I have to do is die.
So when it's my time to kick the pail,
don't nobody take it hard;
Just send my bones to Mr. Jones
and give him my regards.

Throughout the recitation—which was well-lauded at the end —there were nudges and frank nods with murmurs:
"He make that up?"
"Probably."
"He made that up."
"Ain't he a corker?"

"Should be on radio."

Just about then, George made his way back in and stood by the organ at the other end of the mantle. He had a sneaky gleam in his eye. "Okay, Alf, time to give us a step."

"Yeah, come on, Alf," came a voice from the crowd.

"Drive 'er, Alf," Joe Mason said.

Alf's mouth hung open and his eyes faded.

"Well, I'm not much…"

But Jim Mackie and Alban Gallant, with bemused glances at each other, had already hit into a lively reel. Alf rose to his feet, gulped a few times, then began shooting out his feet in a diddle-stomp hobble.

"Yahoo!" Joe Mason hollered. "Drive 'er, Alf."

Then George moved around until he stood in front of Alf and bellowed above the music, "You call that dancing? Look at him—diddly diddly de."

Alf gave George a dirty look and disappeared. Alf held up his hand for the music to stop. "We'll have John and Agnes now with Sally Lutz," he said.

John and Agnes did a decent job on the song, with their heads back and hands clasped behind their backs. Didn't have to be coaxed, either.

After a respectable applause, someone called for a waltz and the dancers found their partners and the musicians played the sweet, haunting strains of "Over the Waves." Wally Mason stood, head hung, in a corner with lament on his face, and I knew what he was feeling: we didn't get our chance to play.

But Linda Robins came from I don't know where and stood in front of Wally and waited for him to make his move.

Wally stood peering up with his head still hung until Linda frankly set her fists into her hips. She stood that way with her lips pursed for a bit, then caught him by both arms and hauled him onto the floor. It took Wally a while to get his feet going, but he did, eventually, with Linda's help. She could move around pretty good, with her chin up and that frank, smug look on her face. She was pretty able, too. By the time I decided to check out the card game in the porch, she had Wally hobbling around pretty good. He even seemed like he was enjoying himself.

The Old Man, Alf Wallace, Joe Mason and John Cobly were having a four-hander of auction. In a shadowy corner in a sunken armchair, Dan Coulter sat, sneaking sips from a cup he would replenish from under his coat. In their off-game banter, without them knowing it entirely, they were about to herald in the second, and what turned out to be the number one, major happening of that spring.

"You really think it'll go through, do you, Dan?" John Cobly said. "I'll bid twenty five."

"Thirty," The Boss said.

"Thirty-for-sixty," John Cobly said, eyeing The Boss.

"Away," The Boss said. "What have you been drinking?"

"Yup," Dan Coulter said. "We'll have it before the fall." Dan's voice had a mellow placidness; the sleepiness of his stare was faded in shadow.

John Cobly gathered up the kitty and changed around the cards in study.

"What makes you think that?" Joe Mason said.

"Hearts are trump," John Cobly said.

"The election's coming off," Dan Coulter said. There was the call for cards, with Alf Wallace flipping them around from the pack.

"Okay, best in your flipper, Joe," John Cobly said. Cards were thumped onto the table in the flurry of lift-taking exchange until one final thump came louder than the rest and John Cobly said, "Take that. Put that in your pipe and smoke it. Sixty spuds mark it up."

"But what's the election got to do with it?" Joe Mason said, gathering the cards, tapping them into a pack and shuffling. "It never made any difference before."

"Fred James bought Albert Leland out and he'll need Hook and that part of Jar running past Harvey's to truck potatoes from the warehouse there to his rail spur."

The four men at the table froze in their positions, their heads snapping as one toward Dan. There was a pause before Joe Mason spoke. "Couldn't he shoot them down to Bob Wayne's spur like they do now?"

"Nope. Fred James ain't selling to another buyer. He means to truck them."

"And he ain't going to truck them without a snowplow, and there'll be no plowing without a decent road," The Boss said in a muse.

"Fred James is going big," Dan Coulter said.

"He's already big," Alf Wallace said.

Dan Coulter held his hands wide. "Bigger. There's property for sale running from Albert's straight through to the county road. It'll be Fred Jones's property in the near future, if not as I speak."

"Think he's got enough pull to bring in the road machines?" Joe Mason said, shuffling the cards absently.

Dan Coulter took another pull from his cup. "Got more pull than everyone on Hook Road put together and then some."

"That's a fact," John Cobly said. "But we'll take her any way she comes. Hey, don't wear the spots off the cards, Joe. Deal up, and don't go to the manure pile."

"How do you know all this?" Alf Wallace said.

Dan Coulter took another pull. "It's written in the wind, boys, written in the wind."

"I asked you not to go to the manure pile, Joe," John Cobly said.

"Mother, I've come home to die," The Boss said.

"Let the whining begin," Joe Mason said.

"Thirty days," Alf Wallace said.

"You got guts," John Cobly said.

"More guts than brains, if his hand is anything like mine," The Boss said.

"Take her home, Alf," Joe Mason said.

"Let's see what's in the kitty..." Alf Wallace said. "Diamonds are trump."

They dropped the subject then. Maybe it was because they were mulling over the fact that the surveyors had come back in the spring and finished staking off the road, or maybe they just didn't believe Dan.

It was hard to place much store in a man's word when he lived like Dan. Dan always drank and did things a bit different. But when his house had burnt down a few years back, and his wife, Lyla, had died from too much smoke, he went to the point of being strange. He didn't bother building a new house—just moved into the porch, which they'd managed to save. He didn't even bother to fix it up—just nailed a few shelves to the wall and hauled in a bed and a table; the pump and sink were already there. It was said that he'd never drawn a completely sober breath since the fire.

But, for all, Dan was well-read and knew more than most and nobody knew for sure whether he got it right because he had the facts, or just figured it out. Whatever the case, two weeks or so later, roaring, rutting and rooting like a square-snouted boar, toppling trees and crowding them into mangled mounds of boles, limbs and stump fans, a fine powder of dust and diesel fumes clouding it, the first Caterpillar began working in Dan's hollow. Then more Caterpillars came, and graders, and they sheared the ground in that determined pace, working in seemingly nowhere directions, until the road, as we knew it, turned to a broad mess of sod mounds, gouges and swerving ruts.

They didn't give us a lot of time to deal with our fences. But we managed to salvage what worthwhile wire and posts we could from our old line before they gathered it up and trucked it away and ran a temporary line, with a post here and there along the pasture field, about halfway down to our north line, to do until we could get the permanent fence in.

We were working on the new fence one afternoon when John Cobly dropped by. I was down in the hole for the new corner post at our gateway, shovelling out what brick clay and stone The Boss had just crowbarred loose. The Boss was leaning on his shovel, watching the action on the road. John Cobly pulled his horse and truck wagon from the maze of clay mounds and ruts into the tip of our lane. The right front wheel of the wagon butted against the round bales of barbed wire lying by the pile of cedar posts the peddler from up west had brought down. From up the road came the clanking rattles and snorts of a bulldozer.

"They're driving 'er, Harv," John Cobly said, raising his voice. He pulled out his makings and began rolling a cigarette.

"They surprised us," The Boss said.

"Yep, makes things look kind of bald, don't it?"

"They can really tear things up. That's good enough, Jake. We might as well put in the corner post."

We went for the anchor post, lying with parallel planks fastened to its big end with spikes and twists of wire, and dropped it into the hole. The Boss held it vertical by its top until I'd shovelled in enough dirt to set it, then he began tamping down the clay with a thin post as I shovelled.

John Cobly sat quietly, watching us and smoking. The horse, fidgeting now and then, had worked its way to a patch of lush grass growing by the pile of posts. Suddenly, it went for the grass and there was the slide of the collar dropping to its ears.

"What's that, four foot deep?" John Cobly said.

"Four and a half; the frost comes pretty heavy here."

"Going to fence her all this summer?"

"No, just this field I'm using for pasture. Do the rest in the fall if I can find the time." The Boss was speaking around the cigarette lodged in the corner of his mouth between pounds of his post.

"Wonder what finally brought them to it?"

"Conservatives got more liquor for votes than usual and made the Liberals shaky, I imagine," John Cobly smirked.

"Maybe what Dan said about Fred James was right."

"Could be, unless it's got something to do with something further down the road. Your progress, maybe."

"Well, if it is, ain't nothing going to stop it."

We finished filling in the hole.

"Think you can dig the hole for the brace post on this side, Jake?" The Boss said. I took the metal rod-handles of the digger—lying near—scissored them open, drove the half-cylinder-like jaws into the ground, forced the handles to and lifted a round junk of sod.

"He's getting 'er, Harv," John Cobly said. "They soon grow up."

"That's the way it goes," The Boss said. "Before too long, instead of him helping me, I'll be helping him."

I began struggling with a junk of stone I had hit into.

"That's all right, Jake, just leave it for now and take a rest," The Boss said. He turned then, his eyes sweeping up the road. "Not going to be the same around here."

"Oh, bit of a change for a while," John Cobly said. "We'll be blessing it when the mud and snow hits."

We all noticed the flashes of blue showing and disappearing amidst the maze up the road. Eventually a late-model car emerged with glints of sun on its grill teeth and its round, bloated fenders. Weaving its way with a lazy bounce, it came to our gateway and tucked in angle-wise behind the wagon.

The man behind the wheel wore a grey fedora with a feather tip in its band and a matching grey suit. His face was lean, with a thin mouth and large eyes that had a constant shift. He stepped out of the car, turned and looked briefly at the roadwork, then walked casually toward us, his right hand taking a bellied lighter and a pack of tailor-mades from his pocket. He paused and lit a cigarette, snapping the lighter's flipper and shielding the flame with his hand. He put the cigarettes and lighter away in a smooth motion and moved closer.

John and The Boss quietly watched him approach, sizing him up.

His words came quick and friendly when he spoke. "You've got a going concern here," he said, blowing out smoke.

"Yeah, they're driving 'er," John Cobly said.

The man turned and looked toward the pasture and the cattle grazing there. "Nice herd of cattle," he said.

"Not bad," The Old Man said. "You a cattle buyer?"

The man glanced at The Boss, dropped his eyes and briefly studied the ground, then looked up, taking a quick suck of his cigarette.

"No, my name's Jim Shirley. I deal in farm machinery, primarily tractors. Wondering if either of you two gentlemen would be interested."

"What breed?" John Cobly said.

"Ferguson," Jim said.

"Never heard of them," John Cobly said.

"They've caught on quite well in other parts," Jim Shirley said, taking a brochure from inside his coat, flicking it open and holding it out like a sign. The brochure's black and white pictures showed a small, squat tractor in front, side and back views.

The Boss put on his glasses and moved with John to get a better look.

"Kind of looks like a Ford," John said.

"Better than a Ford," Jim Shirley said. "Most up-to-date tractor there is. Way ahead of its time, actually: hydraulic transmission, three-point hitch, smoothest power takeoff there is. More horsepower than any other tractor its size."

"What about the Farm-All A?" John said.

"They're a good, tough little tractor, like most of the thirty or so horsepower tractors. They'll all get the job done, but this one is a cut above the rest. Anybody who's tried them will tell you." Jim Shirley was talking fast, his eyes shifting almost in sync with his words.

"What about the price?" John Cobly said.

"Fifty to a hundred dollars more than the others, depending on which one, but they're worth it. And we offer the easiest, simplest financing."

A dump truck roared past and the conversation went on hold until the noise subsided.

"I'm not sure I'll buy a tractor," The Boss said.

"I should think a man your age would be glad to have one," Jim Shirley said.

"They're a great work saver, especially at harrowing and plowing."

"I'm not completely sold on this financing you're so hot about," The Boss said.

"It's like I told you," John Cobly said. "All it'll take is an extra milk cow and another acre of potatoes."

"The way I see it, that it's just the beginning of a bunch of expenses that'll saddle us with a debt we won't be able to handle with what we produce," The Old Man said.

"You're looking at it the wrong way," John Cobly said.

"It'll just be a matter of better farm management enabling you to grow a heavier cash crop, like adding an acre of potatoes and increasing your dairy output," Jim Shirley said.

"I ain't so sure about all this," The Old Man said, canting his head and scratching his chin.

"You'll look cute slaving away with your three horses while everyone is riding high on a tractor, Harv."

"He's right," Jim Shirley said. "We've got the tools to make life easier, put more enjoyment in life."

"I'd sooner slave and make sure my bills are paid so I can get a decent night's sleep."

Jim Shirley went to speak but paused with his eyes shifting from John to The Boss. He was still holding the brochure like a sign, but at about waist level now. His eyes shifted full to John. "What about you, sir?" he said.

"I'll take a brochure," John Cobly said.

Jim Shirley took out a fountain pen and hastily wrote his name and business address on the brochure.

"My office is in town, right by the old bakery," Jim Shirley said, handing the brochure to John Cobly. Without him noticing it, the half-burnt, dead cigarette in his left hand dropped to the ground. "Drop in any time."

"Would you like one, sir?" Jim Shirley said, eyeing The Old Man.

"I'll know where to go if I ever decide."

"And your name, sir?"

"Harvey Jackson."

Jim's eyes turned to John.

"John Cobly."

Jim Shirley shook both men's hands. "Well, they're making progress," Jim said, turning to the roadwork, his words barely audible above an approaching conglomeration of motor bursts and metallic tread knocks. "By the way, who'd be living across the road?" Jim Shirley said, shouting now.

"Joe Mason," John shouted back.

Jim nodded and got into his car.

The dealer started his car seemingly without sound and worked his gearshift and waited, looking over his shoulder while a Caterpillar clunked past, then backed the car onto the road.

We watched the car weave, halt and poke its way through an access path, pause for the Caterpillar on its return, then finally shoot into Joe Mason's lane.

The noise was deafening now. John Cobly just nodded his head at The Old Man and left, too.

We finished digging the hole, put in the anchor and the brace posts, chopped the notches for the brace and spiked it top to bottom between the two posts. The Boss grabbed the puller bar lying on the pile of poles; I grabbed the end of the wire curling close by and jammed it into the flipper-like catch on the puller bar.

The Boss, setting the bar's end hooks against the corner post, with the bar across his thigh, leg-levered it, and the wire strand whipped taut, cuffing up dirt on the mounds by the upright posts spaced down the field to the other corner post. "Might as well run another strand before noon," The Boss said, holding while I stapled on the wire with the claw hammer. He wired out a fresh bale then and held the end to the post while I stapled it. Then he rammed the puller bar through the bale hole and, taking an end of the bar each, we headed down the field with the bale ticking and rolling on the bar between us and the barbed wire trailing off behind.

Prelude to Summer on Hook Road

Regardless of the roadwork, the summer scenes came on as usual on Hook Road. In fine early mornings, the sun, rising above the ragged gloom along the horizon, blazed patches along the cow paths that wound their way through pasture greens like angleworms. The sweet summer smells of new mown hay mingled with the soft summer breezes that faded the lowing of the cows, rising from their rest, stretching stiffly, ambling in their lines through the paths and into the lanes, their ankles cracking, their hooves puffing powdery clay, their long shadows jabbing at the peeling fence posts lining the lanes like guard soldiers with rifles held at ease.

In the stables, the smells of dry manure and sour milk from yesterday's spills mingled with the mists of DDT being sprayed over the cows' backs with plunger-worked sprayers in a fight against the warble fly. Buckets rattled and clanked. Board-made milking stools creaked under the weight of being squatted on. Heads ducked under the casual swish of tail brushes.

At roadside stands, bearing cap-headed, shoulder-gripped cream cans, on their day, came the revving, roaring and stopping of the cream truck.

In the hayfields, the breeze —what there was of it—blew hot, and it seared as much as the sun. The hands of the forkers were calloused as smooth and hard as their fork handles. The forkers would often spit on their hands for grip before sweeping the coils onto the stack-like loads where the builders built, wading, high-stepping and jump-tramping. Over the sheared fields, curlews darted in low, gliding flight, as if cutting through drudgery; horses moped in high-wheeled rakes, the sleepy drivers toeing the trips at the windrow, the half-hooped rake teeth rising tail-like to fall with a *wang*. Through stands of timothy and clover the hay-mowers swept, their cutting bars rattling, their drivers bouncing on stemming seats as if riding something's tail, their horses plodding, with sweat-soaked muscles shining in the sun.

At the barns, the horse-drawn cables ran through pulleys on barn walls and pulleys on the track carriages down to pulleys on the two-tined forks. The workers would plunge into the loads with their feet, then step aside and shout their commands to the horsemen. And a wig-like lift would rise, lock into a carriage and sweep through the loft to fall with the pull of a rope. The fall of a lift would puff cool air at the stowers, standing with sweat pouring down their faces, waiting to wallow in the unsettled hay, fork-pulling at the lift, spreading it, ramming it into corners, gritting, grunting and jump-tramping.

In the potato fields, at intervals, the farmers stalked the drills, searching the tops, bending at times to brush with their hands or root up the "black leg" and the "blight." Sometimes they would spray the potatoes, too, with sprayers that were not much more than a half-barrel on wheels with a pressure pump, a pipe boom and a network of hoses, pipes and end nozzles.

In the evenings, there were games of what could best be termed as "cow pasture ball." Rocks, shingles, junks of board were used for bases, board clubs for bats and usually a sponge ball, which, regardless of its colour, always wound up with a green cast either from cutting through the grass or the odd cow splatter. Care had to be taken not to hit the ball over the fence, especially if the other side was a grain field: you could lose the ball. And it was a good idea to note where the cow splatters lay, for obvious reasons.

Saturday night was the big night. We'd get spruced up to the smells of boughten soap and shoe polish and clatter into town with the lowering sun poking blazes between fence posts and glinting dully on the steel tires of the light wagon.

We'd pull up at the long, open shed with its ever-present smell of horse manure, its roof showing black patches where shingles had blown off. The Boss would tie the mare to the tie rail—gouged by the bites of restless horses—that ran the full length of the back wall, with its gaps from missing boards.

Presently, we'd stand looking into the glass-panelled show-case of the theatre. Usually a gaudily painted man would be looking back with a mysterious eye, the brim of his stetson canting back, a bandana wedging his throat, smoke curling from his brandished six-gun. The smells of popcorn would waft through the open door as we walked through. After getting our thirty-cent ticket at the wicket, we'd pause in the lobby, with its dry stately atmosphere (somewhere between a restaurant and an undertaking parlour) and check out the future billings on the wall.

At the showroom door, the ticket taker looked much like an undertaker, with his sombre expression. Inside the dimly lit room there'd be the murmur of multiple conversations mingling with the sound of the odd pop bottle clunking off the steel seat legs as it wobbled down the slope. We'd flip down a hard seat and sit, waving at familiar face here and there, with bright smiles for the occasion.

Suddenly, the flicker would flash in the flapping rooster as he crowed in the show. Trumpets would blare in the news of the world, with the usual scenes of war and political notables. Gloomy, eerie music would conduct the safari man through his jungle serial and his dealings with bad traders and treasure-seekers, which usually ended with him in a death struggle with a lion or a gorilla (to be continued next week). Somewhere in the preview segments, the singing cowboy would run down a train on his super smart horse, jump a boxcar on the fly, tangle with owl hoots and sing, riding through the sage with his cowgirl.

Then the man with the smoking gun would enter, stalking his way down the dead streets at high noon, his spurs clinking, his right hand poised over the six-gun at his hip. Then came the showdown stare into the eyes of a snake-faced rustler, the flashing quick draw, and Snake Face bites the dust. Then there were the death rattles of more six-guns and lever-action rifles, seasoned with shootouts and riders tumbling from their saddles until a pretty lady got rescued and she and the hero rode into the sunset with THE END at their backs. After the show, we'd be ready to swagger down the streets of Tombstone for a showdown.

But we'd settle for a gallhoot run through the shadowy alleys between the windowless sides of the bank and the funeral parlour. Then we'd swagger out onto the crowded sidewalks of Main Street and coolly greet those we knew and wonder about those we didn't.

Up one sidewalk and down the other we'd go; past the booth, with its smells of steamed clams and hot dogs; past strong, quiet men slouching around shadowy storefronts talking of farm concerns, their black suit coats augmented by the rolled-up cuffs of their new overalls showing white. And through the muddle of bodies onto the sidewalks, the ladies with wave-set hair bustled from shop to shop with their lists.

We'd pause now and then at a store showcase and gaze at the merchandise in the big windows: a shiny bicycle (we'd never own) standing beside an array of axes, picks and shovels in the hardware store; denim jackets hanging in the clothing store above a shelf spaced with boots and folded plaid shirts.

We'd come to the open door of the restaurant with the red-capped stools at a circling counter and rows of booths along its walls. Usually, someone we knew would be in one and we'd go and sit with them and flip through the nickelodeon song leaves in the glassed-in box on the wall while they ate. And the bass-booming songs from the nickelodeon would weave through the buzz and ripple of conversations and there would be the steamy smells of hot hamburg sandwiches and coffee and thick waves of tobacco smoke.

If we had an extra dime, sometimes between the two of us, it would go for a comic at the small shop smelling heavily of the smoked herring that were kept in an open crate with a "five cents each" cardboard tab in their midst. There the proprietor stood, peering through a visor shadow and leaning on a counter cluttered with bubble-gum packs, candy bars and glass jars of candy canes, candy cones and licorice cigars.

The comics were in individual stacks on a back shelf. There would be Kid Long on a cover, standing feet apart with his 45s brandished high, gun smoke wafting around him, his hat behind his shoulders, hanging by the chin laces knotted at his throat. The G Man would be on another cover, in a trench coat, confronting ugly hoodlums with a blazing tommy gun. The combat soldier, advancing through shellfire, firing his rifle from the hip, would grace another cover. And it would be too bad, but you'd have to make a choice and live with it.

Soon it would be ten o'clock and we'd be back at the shed at our prospective wagons. In the shallow glow of a naked bulb on an electric pole we'd mount up and move out. Fleeting shadows would flare at the mare's feet; now and then the glare of a car's lights would sweep, leaving it hard to see. And the town lights would fade, the pavement would break into clay, the darkness would turn the mare into a dark silhouette. We couldn't see the road, but she could and she'd road along making the turns in the darkness until she stood in the barnyard, snorting and waiting to be unhitched.

Summer on Hook Road

CHAPTER 6

The Saturday night trips to town were always highlights, regardless of whatever else did or didn't stick out. That summer there were few other things that did. The road grading stood out, of course, but by the time summer got going anyways decent, we had grown used to the stink, dust and noise and having to either work our way through it or detour when we went somewhere.

Joe Mason was taking a heifer to Young Tom's bull one night and got her tangled up in a road grader. That was interesting. I was heading out with my guitar to play with Wally and I met Joe and the heifer coming out of Joe's gateway. The heifer was hauling Joe, with the rope wrapped behind her ears and muzzled at her nose, her head bent low and back, her nostrils snuffing dust around her front hooves, her mouth belching out mournful bawls, foam and saliva. Joe was leaning back, dragging on his heels, with the rope running around his shoulders and his left hand clutching the lead with his arm straight out. But his lean went too far, either that or he slipped, and his rear end *whumpfed* into the dust in the lane and then Joe was sprawling in a slow turn like a chip in an eddy, his bald head barely visible in a cloud of powdery red clay.

He got turned around enough to butt his feet against a gatepost somehow and the heifer swapped ends in a wild fishtail as she snubbed up, switching her tail with her head low and her eyes mean. Joe tied the rope to the post and hunched with his hands on his knees, breathing heavy. Then he grabbed a hank of grass and attempted to rid his overalls of the dusted green manure he was dragged through. Eventually he shuffled up to the cow's rear end and caught her tail. After a few swipes, and with a sharp twist or two, he got her headed in the right direction. Suddenly, she burst forward and Joe untied the rope on the fly. Away they went, the heifer at a steady trot, Joe loose-roping with his bowed legs churning in a hop, skip and jump. They were making pretty good time until the loose rope end got tangled around Joe's legs—*whumpf!*—and down he went again. There was a windrow of loose clay running along the edge of the road and Joe, refusing to let go of the rope, got dragged through it head first, until the heifer barged under the hoop of the road grader and got the rope tangled up in the shear with her head snubbed into a pile of dirt. There must have been a half-bushel of clay down Joe's overall bib. It took quite a bit of hand flapping, leg shaking and cursing to get things cleared away. I put my guitar down and offered to help.

"Nope," Joe said, "she's good right where she's at." He hobbled down to Young Tom's, still flapping at his pants and cursing, and he and Tom came back with the bull.

Wally and I went to the exhibition that year, on our own for the first time. The Yodelling Cowboy came back again with the champion fiddler. They were playing in the coliseum where they held the stock shows, vaudeville acts and whatever.

While we waited on the train-station platform on a bright August day with a sultry breeze, a couple of truck wagons clattered into the village sleepiness and an old truck rattled through. In a field next to the station, a horse-drawn sprayer blew a fog of mist along its extending booms, its pump pistons thump-sucking regular beats among the spray-hiss and the *clumps* of the horses' footfalls. The diesel engine had been in for a while by then. We didn't pay it much attention when it came square and quiet, emitting its heat waves and diesel stink: it just wasn't a steam engine.

We were the only passengers on the platform and among few in the coach car. An old lady and a young boy sat across the aisle from us. The lady had a straight back and it fit snug against the hard seat. The boy's feet dangled about a foot from the floor and he wore a sailor suit with a pork pie hat, ribbons and all. They were eating fudge from a brown paper bag. Once in a while, the lady turned her face, which was shadowed by a black straw hat, and peered at us through rimless glasses in mid-munch.

The conductor came, swaggering with the sway of the car, and stopped to punch our tickets, the halting snaps muted by wheel rumbles and the *click-clack, click-clack* of the coupling joints. "Where are you young whippersnappers going?" he said, his square, low-set hat brim half hiding his bemused look. We told him. "Be the last they'll see of you two bucks."

Once we got over the excitement, mingled with a mild dose of fear, the feeling of being on our own for the first time, there was nothing to do but watch the scenery go by and put up with the stops, waits and shunts at flag stops and stations. By the time we got to the square city depot, with its slanting canopy, that dry stiffness had set in.

We got directions from a shaggy old man with dirty porcupine quill whiskers set in a bloated face, his faded, bloodshot eyes peering out from beneath the brim of a rumbled slouch hat. He worked a tobacco cud a few times, spat into a cuspidor by the bench he sat on outside of the station and flung his arm sideways in a point. "Follow that street until you see the Ferris wheel," he said in a gravely growl. "And if you don't come back, write."

The grounds were just shaking up when we handed in our quarters at the entrance booth and stepped in. A roustabout in oil-stained jeans and a torn T-shirt,was testing the bell ringer, setting the peg a certain way and swinging the steel-bound wooden maul with grunts. We stood and watched the cube-like slide go up and down the long, flat pole until it finally dinged the saucer-like bell on top. Over by the stage for the girlie show demonstration, one of the girls stood in curlers and a housecoat, taking sucks at a cigarette veed between her fingers. Regardless of the caked-on makeup, which was wrinkled and down-slashed around her eyes and lips, her face was jaded and pale. Just above the board fence at the edge of the grounds, through the shadow of the towering grandstand, the necks and heads of racehorses, with their checkreins and blind bridles, sailed past in exercise, the quick, flat patter of their hoofbeats coming in staccato through the quiet.

Wally tried his luck at catching a prize with one of those crane affairs in a glass cubical. He got his quarter stuck in the chute and he stuck his hand through a little open side door and jiggled it. Suddenly this big heavy jawed Italian came out of nowhere and grabbed his hand. "I got you; you go to jail," the man said.

I don't think Wally wet his pants—maybe a few drops. We did a bit of spluttering to convince him of the facts, and he finally let us go with a warning and a black look.

We staggered around the grounds then, taking in the usual midway scene for a while. We didn't have much more than enough money for the train trip home, so we wound up sitting in the cool, deadened sanctity of the coliseum, watching the stock judging and waiting for the vaudeville acts, which were to be followed by the Yodelling Cowboy. The vaudeville acts came on and performed to the blare of horns and suspended snare-drum rolls with their punctuating bops: the jugglers, unicycle drivers and wire walkers; the bikini clad lady, with her whip and poodles that pranced, rolled drums and jumped through hoops; the clown, with a red nose ball and hair sprigging around a cracker box hat, who roared around in a little car that blew smoke and backfired.

Finally, the Yodelling Cowboy came on. The fiddler didn't look at all like I thought he would. I had him pictured as a stately man with slim hands with long fingers. When I saw this big, blocky man with ham-like hands and banana fingers walking around the stage before the show, sawing segments on a fiddle, I thought maybe he was a stagehand fooling around. But it was him, all right, and when he did his own hit tunes of sweet two-steps and compelling breakdowns— different, a cut above the rest—the strains filled the coliseum, captivating the audience. The staple songs of the Yodelling Cowboy and the lesser songs of the backup crew, augmented by country corn skits and jokes, paled before him, as far as I was concerned. The only thing I noticed about the guitar players was that they didn't go up and down their guitar necks like Alban Gallant.

Wally sat with his face in kind of a delirium, his mouth open and his eyes sticking out. A pretty blonde attendant was selling pictures of the band members at the stage at intermission and Wally bought one of the fiddler and got him to autograph it. He quietly took Wally's picture from his squat on the stage's lip.

"Could you put that 'To Wally'?"

"Okay," the fiddler said in a quiet, sincere voice.

"I play the fiddle, too."

"Do you? How long have you been playing?"

"Little over a year."

"Well, always nice to meet a fellow fiddler."

"I hope to be as good as you some day."

"I'm sure you will. I'll remember your name. We'll probably meet again. Good luck." He shook Wally's hand.

Wally kept looking over his shoulder at him as we walked away and got tangled up in a pile of empty chairs.

Things got kind of interesting after the show. Wally was

hanging back, getting a last look at the fiddler and I guess I was, too, and we forgot that the train would be leaving around the end of the show, at six. By the time I noticed the watch nestled in the red hairs of a stout arm on my left, its hands said five after six. Wally's mouth hung open when I pointed it out, and he gulped with that eye-bug of his.

"Now what do we do?" he said.

"Try to find someone from home and bum a ride, I guess."

The whole thing got kind of strange then. Tiredness was setting in with the lengthening shadows, and we'd had nothing to eat but a hot dog since noon. The muddle of laughter, screams, Crown and Anchor clinks and hawker calls, interspersed with the motor bursts of the rides, amidst the dust and smells, were beginning to blend together with a sultry gloom.

Wally kicked a tent peg and snarled, "Of course there wouldn't be anyone here we know. Of course not. Stupid trains. We should have stayed home."

"Well it was you that wanted to come and see your fiddler, and you that hung around mooning over him until it was too late," I said.

"I didn't twist no arms. I didn't twist no arms."

"Looks like we'll be twisting thumbs."

"Huh? You mean hitchhike?" Wally gulped and went bug-eyed again. "I ain't never done that."

"We'll never learn younger," I said.

Wally curled his lip into a snarl and gave me a sidelong leer. Then his eyes bugged again and his mouth dropped. "Where do we go?" he said in a weak voice.

We got directions and made our way toward the main road out of town. The streets appeared dirty and grey now. Loose papers and candy-bar wrappers skittered along the cracked and stained sidewalks in the sultry breeze. After a few miscues due to direction confusions, we finally got our thumbs up by the long, dirty-grey ribbon leading toward home. We stood between staying and bolting. After some of the terror subsided a bit, I started noticing that the oncoming drivers were giving us blank stares.

Then a big red-headed guy stuck his head out of his car window, glared at us and hollered, "Get over on this side."

We crossed the street hoping for better, but the steady stream of cars went by in that moping parade. The long shadows quenched the sun's last blazes, and everything fell into the dirty greyness of the sidewalks. The air grew sticky in the sultry breeze. I had that stranded feeling. Up ahead, three other young fellows, much like us, came onto the sidewalk and started thumbing, too, in a backpedal.

"What are we going to do if we don't get a ride?" Wally said.

"I don't know," I said. With the cars going by in a relentless stream, and the drivers passively paying us no mind, what hope we had that wasn't drowned by fear was rapidly fading.

When a car finally swerved in and stopped, we stood gaping for a while, unsure of what to do. Then a girl with a pert face, framed by brown hair, stuck her head out the front passenger window and beckoned with a flutter of her hand. We ran then and scrambled and fumbled our way into the back seat of the medium-old car. There were two girls in the front seat, beside the driver, who was a conventional-looking sport with a brush cut.

"Where are you boys going?" the outside girl said.

We told her.

"Not far from Summerside, right?" the guy said, watching for his chance to get back into traffic.

We agreed.

I could see him smirk in the mirror. "I'm an old bus driver."

"Not that old," the middle girl said.

"We'll get youse close," the guy said.

We got underway again and I was just beginning to feel secure when I heard the outside girl picking at the guy in motherly tones: "Ah, come on, pick the poor little fellows up."

"What do you think I am, a bus driver?" the guy growled.

"That's what you just said," the inside girl said.

The guy grudgingly pulled over and the three other hitch-hikers crowded in on us. But they didn't go far.

The driver guy lost his good humour for a while, but the girls, teasing and joking like two pigeons, brought it back. The middle one would break into a current country song now and then in a pleasant voice. They were all in their late teens or early twenties and you could tell by their light banter that they were either out for a joyride or headed for a dance.

Home was about two miles from where they dropped us off. What a relief! To say the least. Wally gave a little dance and started jigging "The Flowers of Edinburgh."

I didn't feel much like a wing-wang—too lank.

"I'll have that one down pretty soon," Wally said. "Time we got at it again." We hadn't been playing that much, what with the work and fishing and one thing or another.

Dan Coulter came visiting one evening, sober for once, about the only other happening worth mentioning that summer. He and The Old Man sat in the kitchen mulling things over, chewing tobacco and spitting into tin cans. Dan didn't care too much for smoking; said it was bad for your constitution. It didn't take them long to get into the roadwork, and they weren't into that long before they were into change.

Dan usually thought a few minutes about something —with those big, musing eyes of his fixed on something and his right eyebrow cocked—before he'd speak. Then he'd spit and out with it.

"Things don't look the same anymore," The Boss said. "Don't even feel the same anymore. Makes you wonder what's going to become of the place."

Dan stared at the stove awhile before the spit came. "Not hard to figure some of it out. As far as the new road is concerned, it's not so much about how it looks, but what it represents—what's going to come with it. It's representing progress, something neither of us is any ways used to, something we haven't seen much of in our lifetime. And progress means change and you're never sure where change will wind up taking you, especially if it comes quick, and it's going to come quick and mostly because people want it. We might as well face it; nobody in their right mind is going to keep to the old ways if he can get out of it—too much like slavery."

"We had it a lot harder than they have today and it never killed us," The Boss said. "Back in the Depression, I cut two team-loads of wood and hauled it out for forty cents a day. They already have it too easy. If they had to wear their socks five ways to keep a patch at the heel, or run beside a sleigh load of mud with nothing but coarse boots on their feet to keep them from freezing, , they'd have something to complain about. But we were happy enough then. It was enough to have a roof over your head and a bite to eat then."

The pause came, then the *punk* in Dan's can. "Didn't know any better then. Things are coming clearer now, though."

The Old Man put down his can and rose and lit the lamp.

"Where's Ella this evening?"

"Over at Joe's. Where do thinks it's all going to wind up?" The Boss said, sitting back down and spitting into his can.

"Tractors will come with whatever, and electricity probably, this and that, less work, more bills, more headaches, more time to get into hellery. All part of progress. Hard to say where it'll go from there. One thing for sure: when progress comes, if you don't change on your own, it'll do the changing for you."

"What about you? You thinking about going tractor?"

Dan Coulter *spitooed* his cud into his can, set the can on the floor and bent over, resting his forearms on his knees. "Not sure what I'll do. Might be best to hang on as long as I can with what I got, then maybe sell out. I'm kind of like you: getting to be too old of a dog for new tricks."

There was a long pause. In a distant pasture, a cow lowed. The old house creaked. The Old Man spit his cud into his can and set it down.

"Don't seem too long ago since we were using the horsepowers," The Boss said quietly, breaking the silence.

"Never seen one of them for a while."

"I mind the day we got our engine. They were showing us how the thing worked, and Willard Wallace was over. They had the thing going and Willard thought he'd take a leak; he wasn't watching where he was aiming—he'd been lifting a few—and he hit the spark plug."

"That would wake him up," Dan Coulter said with a smirk

"Yeh, let a howl out of him. Danced around a bit. Old John Cane was around that day, too. 'They're no good,' he said, 'never take the place of the horsepower—sparks flying, burn the barn down.' Now, it's the tractor."

"Goes in cycles, I guess," Dan Coulter said. "I guess the only fellow that saw it coming was Fred James; he's been getting set for it for a while. You can't fault him for it; he's a good businessman, all part of progress. Good man, too. Mind when things went to pieces on me. Didn't know how I'd get me grain in, and didn't he send his whole crew in one day, put the grain up, never said so much as an I, yes, or no about getting paid back."

"No, and he never will. No. Nothing wrong with Fred James."

The two men fell silent. You could tell by the mood of things that they'd taken the subject as far as they could, either that or as far as they wanted to.

Finally, Dan Coulter sighed and straightened in his chair. "She's going," he said in melancholy tones. "She's going and that's the way she goes." He sighed again and worked his shoulders a few times to shake himself loose. "Wonder if I could get the lend of your scythe? Bunch of weeds growed up before me binder house, want to clear them away."

"Sure," The Boss said, reaching for a carborundum lying

on the radio shelf. "You'll need this. It's a bit dull. It's out in the shop."

The two men went outside. Presently, I could hear their voices somewhat mute just outside the door:

"Not too many of these around, either," The Boss said.

"Nope. They had their day, too. Thanks, Harv. We'll be seeing you."

"Night, Dan. No hurry with that."

Prelude to The Last Set on Hook Road

They finished the road grading when the grain was a patchwork of grey and gold and the chill of another harvest time was in the air. One day, the busy, shunting, roaring machines, billowing up dust and stink, were gone and the road lay a red open wound. Where it used to appear inconspicuous, part of the landscape, now it was high, wide and dominating. A wagon rig travelled it now in insignificance.

The small, easily financed tractors with attached pulleys came on then, essentially with a trip plow and usually a trailer. As an added convenient conveyance, for those who hung back on getting a car, a two-by-four platform could be spiked together to fit on a tractor's draw bar. Blower attachments were obtained for threshers to blow straw into lofts from outside the barn so threshing could be done in the fall instead of in the winter. The poles of the horse-drawn implements were shortened and fitted with draw-bar attachments. There were the roars of motors now, mingling with the thwacks of binder kickers and the rattles of cutting bars. With the high, wide, well-graded road, the slough holes, runoffs and quagmires ceased in spring and fall; in winter, the new snowplows came and kept Hook Road open. You could even have your lane plowed to move your produce.

Stationary engines went then, some for junk, some simply hauled to vacant spots behind the barn or in the woods and left to rust. In their usual, noble obedience, the proud horses began to leave. Usually one was kept for a backup, to haul out manure and wood in the winter—tractors were useless in heavy snow. The rest went for tractor trade-ins, fox meat, leather and glue.

The winter road through the fences, fields, barnyards and sometimes on the road was gone. The rattles of wagon wheels and clops of horses' hooves in the little town on Saturday nights, for the most part, died. It became more and more the thing to slip into town on any given day for a roast of beef, or pork or whatever. Pork barrelling, butter churning, canning and cold storage ceased; frozen carcasses no longer hung in winter woodsheds. Potted meat disappeared.

In cadence with the change sweep, electric light poles came to space along Hook Road. In natural progression, compact pumps came to force water through pipe networks and take away the burdens of hand pumps and the chill of outhouses; washing machines came to take away the drudgery of a washboard, or something pumped or cranked; fridges came to preserve leftovers and keep them from flies and the mustiness of a cellar; new lighting came to brighten a room beyond the shallow glow of a kerosene lamp.

The conveniences allowed for more leisure time, primarily for TV, that box of marvellous flick that came to grace a corner of most every living room, where people sat out their evenings awestruck, their eyes beholding things they had previously only heard of. Now we could see our hockey heroes up close and personal, the comedy and variety shows, duster serials. Hand in hand with TV, subtly weaving its way through the community spirit, the strange, new sound of rock and roll began to lure the youth toward a song and dance our forefathers could not have dreamed off.

Along with all these, gas trucks came on regular runs to fill the squat tanks and to drop off cases of oil and grease. And, in ever-growing volume, the neatly typed bill envelopes came to stuff the mailboxes.

The Last Set on Hook Road

CHAPTER 7

The sallowness of first light added to the depression of having to go to work in the potato field on a gloomy, cold morning. Standing between our mailbox and cream-can stand, waiting for Wally Mason to join me for the pickup from one of Fred James's trucks, my mind began sifting through the changes of the past two years.

Wally Mason was going to school now, like a lot of other rural scholars, a natural upgrading factor since the town had opened for high school. The rest took what they thought they needed from the village school, or what they could handle as far as education went, and packed it in. I was one of those. I'd begun grade nine, but standing in the schoolyard that September, with most of the old crew gone, and work to do at home, I'd had little heart for study anymore.

Hiring out at potato digging, once we got our own crop in, was always a necessity for me, for clothes and pocket money and whatever. It was something new for Wally, though. Joe had always handed him whatever he needed and Wally had done what he could around home at his own pace, which wasn't all that brisk.

But Wally was staying in town with an aunt now while he went to school, and it was difficult to hit Joe up for money, since Joe, like most everyone else on Hook Road, was finding loose change and low bills more and more hard to come by.

This was the third fall now since they'd finished upgrading Hook Road. Outside of the things that had converged from that time: the tractors, cars, electricity, and their spinoffs—and the fact that The Boss would have none of them—there were two major happenings that overshadowed the rest. Those pertained for the most part to my personal realm: we had our wagon smashed up by a car and Wally Mason and I finally got our big chance to play.

The accident happened on our way home from a Saturday-night trip to town two summers previous. Because of the increase in car traffic, it was no longer safe to travel by wagon on the main road; we were on the Able Road that tees off the east end of Jar and meanders with a lot of crooks and turns before connecting with the front road at the outskirts of town. We were about halfway between the town road and Jar, coming into a long sweep with a sudden twist at the end. I was standing on the kick, holding onto the seatback. You could just see a dim outline of the mare. The rattles and engine flubs of an old car broke into the mare's foot thuds and the clatter of the light wagon with ever-increasing volume until, with a sudden sweep, the car's lights glared around the turn, half blinding us. Because of the sharpness of the turn, the car was on us before we knew it, and I caught the dark form of the mare shying sideways with the sudden glare.

Almost immediate with the crunching sound of steel hitting wooden spokes, I felt the bushes of the ditch rustle and poke at me as I thudded in. Then there was the scrape of wagon wheels on the hard roadbed, gnashing with the angry revs of the car's engine. I wound up on my side, fighting to catch my breath. Through wheel spokes and dust, I could see the car's light beams halt, reverse, halt again, then shoot ahead until there was the red nub of the car's rear light disappearing into dust and darkness.

It took The Old Man some time to settle the mare down. When he called to me, I was barely able to answer. I'd had my wind knocked out pretty bad, but I was all right.

"Looks like the front wheel is smashed out of shape, and all because some stupid ass wasn't watching what he was doing," The Boss said as I made my way out of the ditch.

"Could have gotten us killed," Nanny said from the seat. "Will the wheel get us home?"

"Going to have to, one way or another."

We came home that night with the left front wheel wobbling in a series of scrapes, drags and thumps.

It was to be our last Saturday-night trip to town by light wagon. Wally Mason and I took to hitchhiking rides to town. The Boss and Nanny would go to the city with Joe and Mabel in their car, a trip that changed to Friday nights with the new shopping hours that came in a little over a year ago.

The big chance for Fiddling Wally Mason and Picking Jake Jackson ended up in much the same shape as our light wagon. We had been practising faithfully under the inspiration from meeting the fiddle champion, waiting for our big break.

We'd decided not to go in the Christmas concert. I guess that's self-explanatory. Then, the previous summer, Enzer Reeves and Holly Macdonald had gotten married and they'd held the tyme in the hall. Jim Mackie had gotten his bow-arm bunged up when he'd got it caught in his tractor's power takeoff, and him and Alban Gallant had decided to hand things over to us.

The whole shebang was a disaster, really. Right from the start there was a strangeness hanging around, with nobody knowing what to do. It seemed that people had lost touch from not talking enough and spending too much time watching TV. When they finally warmed up, the things that needed saying, having built up for quite a spell, began bursting out in a conglomeration of volleys and kept getting louder until you couldn't hear yourself think.

When it came time to start the proceedings, Caleb Johnston, the one heading things up, couldn't get everyone to shut up. After coming to the point of yelling at them, with no let-up, he stiffened his neck into a bow, stomped down to the basement and came back with the galvanized washtub they used for dish washing and a dipper. I guess he must have banged the tub for a good five minutes, hollering as well, until the buzz gradually began to break, with the odd person ducking toward somebody for a last word then sitting up straight like they just stole something. Caleb managed to get the gifts presented and the address read, between cautions, then called for the dance, introducing Fiddling Wally Mason and Picking Jake Jackson.

We started off, but those who had not lapsed into conversation sat mummified, shooting vacant glances at one another.

"Come on," Caleb roared. "That's good music. Grab your partner."

A few stood up as if hanging on the edge, waiting for a lead.

"That's it," Caleb said. "Get up here! That's good music." At times Caleb would turn to us. "Keep going," he'd say. "Once we get them moving, they'll go."

They finally did, a few; but it was more half-hearted flounder than anything else. Those old enough to know how it was done hadn't much heart for it, for whatever reason (could be the music had something to do with it); those younger, the ones that bothered, didn't have it down that good and didn't have much heart for it, either. They got mixed up at the grand chain, flat-footed at the swing, their feet moving in a stiff, reluctant shuffle. It all petered out before the set was over, and Wally and I quit playing and sat wondering what to do.

Then Jerry Jacobs took the floor with his guitar and started singing and banging the strings, dipping the guitar neck, rocking and wiggling while he sang, his tongue flapping around his big buck teeth at certain words, his big blue eyes staring. Then some of the teens got up and began dipping and twirling in that pull-hand scuffle. Soon more were into it, while Wally and I sat with our instruments on our laps like two whipped dogs.

The older people, and the married young, began to drift outside into a medium-cool evening—to stand talking of things of yesterday, change, tomorrow. Those caught in between young and old, the singles, after wondering what to do for a while, wandered outside, too—the men to talk in their group of car makes, wild rides and lemons; the ladies in their group to talk about who was going with who, hairdos and gossip, with the odd glance being exchanged between groups, some suggestive of a ride home.

That was it for Wally.

He put his fiddle and bow, potato sack and all, into the attic. I kept picking the guitar some; tried singing a few times, country songs and whatnot. But you may as well say that the musical dreams of Fiddling Wally Mason and Picking Jake Jackson went up in smoke from the fire of Rocking Jerry Jacobs and his guitar.

Wally's foot shuffles, coming dry and vacant from Joe Mason's lane, brought me back to the present. His skinny frame loomed through the gloom. He was hunched over, with a lunch box under his arm. He shuffled to a halt beside me. "Cold," he said at my greeting, driving his hands into his pockets and hunching all the more.

From the village way, the rattles and roar of a truck broke in and grew louder until we could see the weaves and jiggles of the twin lights topping the rise at the hollow.

"Here they come," Wally said, somewhat gloomily.

The lights bore down on us and came to a stop; the idle of the motor muted in that hic and chug. Arms reached from the high tail end of the truck and hauled us up.

Wally forgot about the lunch can under his arm when he was pulled up and we could hear it clatter on the road. "Go ahead," someone yelled. The truck roared and lurched ahead and we grabbed for its racks. "Hold her, he dropped his lunch can," came another voice and there were thumps on the cab until the motor fell, the brakes screeched and Wally and I went barrelling into a group of bodies huddled against the cab.

One of the warehouse men dropped over the tailgate, then vaulted back up on his hands and groped toward Wally. "Here," he said. "Put this thing in your ear."

"Let 'er rip," came another yell.

With the chill breeze sucking in at us, we roared down to Jar and, after a pulling swerve, we headed down to its end, tucked into the short lane and halted by the warehouse. In the greying light, regular hands—in their shapes, sizes, ages and colours of dress—from our truck or the truck from the other direction, walked stiffly either to the warehouse or to the tractors with attached trailers, sitting half hidden in gloom in the yard. The truck moved on slowly, rocking and bumping with the engine subdued, until one it made one final rock with a bump and the engine cut. We piled off the tail end, our feet driving into the soft clay of the potato field, and headed for a huge pile of baskets nearby.

We huddled then, murmuring in clipped tones through chattering teeth, and got our baskets while the straw boss got our names. Up the field, stepping off the distance with measured strides, his mouth mutely working with his count, the foreman was making his way toward us. There were close to fifty of us, mostly women or school kids let out for the harvest break. We followed the foreman back down like a gaggle of geese, with him poking down the section stakes at intervals, and us dropping off in pairs at our sections. Along the verge of the un-dug rows, a loader-man kneeled on the tail of a trailer, hauled by a sleek green tractor, and threw off empty bags in a ragged line. A ways over, in the rows still crowned with dead sprigs, came the *carrump* of a tractor-hauled topper with a low, humped back as it beat its way up the rows. From the headland came the sudden barks of an ancient tractor, its makeup of steel, cleated rear wheels, disc-like front wheels, sparse engine, hay-mower–style seat and vertical steering wheel, looking like it had escaped from a junkyard more than once.

After the barks stuttered a bit, in a *rutt, rutt, rutt,* the creaks and rattles of the connected two-row digger broke in and the combination began its creep up the rows. The noise of the barks, rattles and creaks was deafening as it passed our section stake, with the mix of tops, stones, potatoes, clay and clods spewing over the digger's tail; the digger-man on his seat poking with a rod to keep the flow running on the chain beneath him; the tractor driver glancing behind and down at times to check the run of the power takeoff.

It took Wally a while to get shook out. The field was over a mile long; the sections were seventy yards or more. It was daunting to look down to the other stake, which Wally did. He wound up standing bewildered for a while, fooling around with his gloves. I had to help him get picked up on the first couple of passes.

"You're going to have to bear down, Wally," I said. "Once

you get behind, you'll never get caught up."

"I don't feel so good," Wally said. "I think I got the flu."

Then Linda Robins, who just *happened* to get the next section up from ours with Janet Fuller, began to crow: "Wally's getting behind, Wally's getting behind. Poor old slow poke Wally; have to go and get his Mommy to help him."

Johnny Ray sang out from the trailer he was loading on. "Come on, Wally, don't let them laugh at you like that. Pull out the blue rag."

When I glanced back at Wally again, he had a mean look in his eye; his jaw was jutting and his hands were milling in tune with the waggle of his backside. It wasn't long before I heard him scratching and snuffing and closing in on me. "Get out of me road," he said, hedging past. "I'll show you how to pick the doggone potatoes."

By mid-morning, we had broken into the work rhythm. Before noon, we were able to gain enough rest between sets to sit and watch the men load the trailers or get a drink from the cream can of water they carried.

The sudden cease of the old tractor's barks, signalling the noon break, brought things to an eerie quiet. The wind was low, cuffing up just a hint of dirt. We sat behind a shelter of filled bags we'd set up and opened our lunch cans. I was just getting into a sandwich when Wally let out a curse. When I looked, he was staring, head bent, at a broken bottle and some milk-soaked sandwiches in his lunch can. When he finally stopped cursing, he held up a sandwich, paused for the drip to stop, then—with his head back and his mouth open—he lowered down a corner and bit in. The milk oozed around his lips and dribbled off his chin. I almost choked.

"Go ahead and laugh; go ahead and laugh," he said, his words gagging. "What a man has to go through in this world."

We settled down to rest leeward behind the bags when we got lunch out of the way. There was just enough chill in the breeze to make the sun a comfort; we lay back feeling the after-lunch laziness setting in with its stiffness. The girls lay on their set with their feet pointing up and toward us, their slanting faces half shadowed by their bandana peaks. We could hear their low melodic murmurs mingling with the cries of a flock of curlews skimming into a nearby pasture field.

"We should visit the girls," I said.

Wally pried an eye open and glanced their way. "Go ahead. If you don't come back, write."

We fell into a drowsy silence for a while.

"You know there's got to be a better way of doing this," Wally broke in.

"Here we go."

"No, but there's got to be a better way."

"Mechanical pickers."

"Nah, they're no good, too slow. Can't grade out all the tops and rocks at any decent speed; more stopping and starting than you can shake a stick at; half the time the man at the end can't keep the bags from running over. Kept me busy cleaning up after the old man's. No good for Fred James, that's for sure. He'd need a dozen or more with the five hundred acres he's got."

Wally paused, sifting clay with his fingers. When he spoke, his voice took on a far-off idle tone. "Way I see it you could take a big funnel and drag it behind the digger 'til it gets full, then hang it up and dump it into dump trucks from the small end."

"With a steam crane and a sky hook. And thirteen bulldozers to haul it down the field."

"Ten would do."

"Then what would we do?"

"Drive a bulldozer."

"Who could afford it?"

"Well, there's that," Wally said. "We couldn't, that's for sure. We're at the point of needing a bigger mailbox now with all the bills coming our way."

"Joe feeling the pinch pretty bad?"

"Most everybody is, except youse. Think Harvey will ever change, get a tractor, the lights and that?"

"Hard to tell what goes on with The Old Man most often. He's getting old, though, no two ways about that. We may not be getting the bills, but the slaving and doing without could be getting to him. Shipped his potatoes out by truck last winter. He'll even sneak a visit to someplace where there's a TV to watch the fights or a hockey game. I guess it's like Dan Coulter says, 'If you don't change with progress, it'll do it for you.' And the rheumatism is hitting The Boss pretty good now, too. But you never know; he's a tough, stubborn old bird."

The wind began to pick up; a sudden whirl flapped a loose bag mouth, belting us with a choky puff. Two guys a few sections down were punch-sticking potatoes to the end of short sticks and whipping them across the field at a flock of seagulls. Up and down the fields, pickers were limp-footing across the drills to and from a woods nearby on toilet breaks.

"When do we get paid?" Wally said.

"Saturday afternoon. They hold back a day's pay."

"Three day's pay, fifteen bucks. I'll have me a hot hamburg sandwich and a banana split at the restaurant, thank you very much."

"*Big Plane Riders* is on. Should be a good movie. I'm wondering how The Marshal's going to make out in the showdown with the gunfighter in the serial."

"Coming over to watch *Durango* tonight?"

"Might. How's school, by the way?"

"Not bad. Some nice girls."

"Pull a Casanova yet?"

"I am Casanova."

The sudden, sputtering *rhutt, rhutt, rhutt* of the tractor's barks broke in from the headland.

"Bark, you pile of junk," Wally said, sitting up. Then he jumped to his feet with a curse. "Got to go. Flying axe handles—must have been something from the lunch can got into me lunch." He cursed again bounded up and limp-footed across the drills, glancing over his shoulder at the digger at times.

I met up with Wally that Saturday night in the Masons' porch. He was gluing his hair back in front of the mirror over the sink, with that goo women used to set their hair with. Wally's hair was never meant to be combed back, but since he'd started school in town, he wouldn't have it any other way. Trouble was, once the goo dried stiff, the hair would spring up in thick points and he'd look like a kingfisher. It seemed in tune somehow, though, when you considered his black suit, short at the arms and legs, his green shirt, red tie and wool socks and those big feet of his.

We had been hitchhiking pretty regular that summer, but the wind was cold that night and we'd decided to catch a ride with Dan Coulter in the old rattle trap he had recently obtained. Dan was eating supper by the light of one low-watt bulb hanging from an open rafter when we got to his house.

His shadow pretty much covered the few dishes scattered in a ragged semi-circle on the naked top of his table. At the far side of the bare wood floor, across from where the kitchen range sat, shaggy and slightly awry from its flue pipe, a floor TV sat below three rough-board wall shelves stacked with books.

It was known that Dan had been drinking less since he got the TV. But you could tell by the slurs in his speech, the jerky way he spooned his stew, the long slurps as he ate, that he wasn't exactly on the wagon.

"You fellows want some stew?" he said.

I was full of Saturday night beans so I decided against it.

"I'll have some," Wally said. That was another thing about Wally: he eat could anytime, anywhere and as much as he liked and he wasn't much more than skin and bones.

Dan flung out his arm in mid-slurp and pointed to some extra dishes and cutlery in the oven. Wally got a bowl and helped himself to the stew from a large, gravy-encrusted pot on the stove. Then he sat down across the table from Dan and began poking it back like he hadn't had supper, or dinner either.

"That's good," Wally said without looking up. "Partridge, eh?"

I was standing behind Wally, and Dan bobbed his head sideways so he could see me. A clownish grin crossed his face and screwed up into a delayed wink.

"Nope, it's muskrat."

"Yeah, ha, ha, muskrat," Wally said. "That's funny."

"Nothing funny about it," Dan said in a fuzzy drawl. "It's a big, fat muskrat—they make the best stew. The thin ones are better fried."

Wally's head tilted up and his hand, with a spoon full of stew, froze about halfway up to his mouth.

Dan flung his arm out and pointed to a pelt hanging on a bare wall stud. "It's muskrat," he said.

Wally reeled from his chair, gagging out, "Muskrat!" Then he wobbled to the door, stuck his head out and hocked and heaved with his knees half bent.

"That mean you don't like muskrat?" Dan slurred.

Not a trapper himself, Wally couldn't reason that the pelt was from last year's catch. Trapping season wouldn't open for a week or so.

We got away, with Dan Coulter stiff-arming the wheel of his old square car, his long neck stiffened into a bow. Eventually, after hedging the ditch here and there, and nearly sideswiping a light pole, we made it to town. Dan pulled up at a curb not far from what was left of the horse shed. The car backfired when he cut the motor and a weave of blue smoke, barely visible from the glow of a streetlight, wafted under his nose.

"Well, me boys, we made her in and we'll make her out, the good Lord willing," Dan said. "Should meet here around ten I guess." A wry, somewhat mischievous, look came over his face. "We'll wait on one another whatever."

With only a few people scurrying here and there and what few cars were parked, the street had a cold, vacant look. There were no wagon wheels jutting into the pale light at the horse shed. The hot dog stand was a black block amidst the taller buildings.

There were a lot of empty seats at the theatre and the vacant dryness gave a depressing effect to a half-decent movie.

The wind had picked up by the time the movie was over; it moaned and whistled around the storefronts and rocked the telegraph and electrical wires. A heavier chill had moved in and, with the moan of the wind, the dim, near-vacant streets gave off an eerie oppression. There was a dry quietness inside the stores now, with the proprietors and attendants watching, strikingly inanimate and almost doleful, some with one foot on a stool or a chair and arms draping at the knee.

After checking a few prices here and there, we decided that sometime soon we'd go to the city—where things were cheaper and more varied and there was some life—to buy most of our wares. While we were in town, I bought a smoked fish and Wally got a current gossip magazine with a girl in a bikini on most every page. The proprietor in the little store stood in quietness as well, in his usual pose, peering at us from under his visor.

"Quiet tonight," I said.

"Getting quieter all the time," the proprietor said.

"Too much TV," I said.

"TV, cars and the stores opening on Friday nights in the city. The town is drying up. Ben's going to close the restaurant in a week or so. Hal is talking about closing his clothing store. There's talk of them closing the feed mill, too. And I'm just getting by by the skin of me teeth. Thank you very much."

There wasn't much of a buzz in the restaurant; the smells were still there and the bass sound still thumped from the nickelodeon. But there was no trouble finding a seat.

"When are we going to the city?" I said.

"Might as well go next Friday night."

"Hitchhike?"

"Might as well."

"We could take in the hop at the rink—last night before they freeze the ice."

Wally shot a sour look at me bordering on betrayal. "You really listen to that junk?" He moved back, still eying me with that sour look, as the waitress set down our hot hamburg sandwiches.

"Turn on the radio, baby-o, and let's rock and roll. I've been tuning in most of the summer, ever since they started playing the hop on the radio."

"Ah, you're spoiling me hot hamburg sandwich. Ugh, you're even starting to sound like them. Dear, dear, dear."

"Ah, just a passing thing, Wally. That's what The Boss says."

Wally went completely rigid and dropped his fork. "Ah, dear, spoil a man's appetite."

"Maybe you should try it; be the first to rock on the fiddle—

Rocking Wally with his rocking fiddle. Got to change with the times, Wally."

Wally shook his head and finished his hot hamburg sandwich without looking at me.

"That ain't the biggest banana split I've seen," Wally said when the waitress brought it around.

"That's okay," she said. "You're not a very big monkey."

We were surprised when we saw Dan Coulter's rangy, square-shouldered, long-headed frame, silhouetted by street lights, come heading for the car slightly before ten.

He wobbled his way to the driver's side and stood, swaying and fumbling for his keys. "Evening, fellows," he grunted when we spoke to him. It took quite a while for him to get behind the wheel; he sat rigid for a while longer before he spoke over his shoulder to us in the back seat. "Boys, I must confess that I'm about three quarters in the bag due to a little over-partaking. Now, I think there's a possibility that I might be able to run this machine, but I'm a little doubtful if I'm able to steer this tin fizzy on me own. Now the way I got it figured, if one of youse got in the front beside me to keep an eye on the road, and if the other reached over me from the back and steered, I should be able to handle the gears and gas and hopefully the brakes."

"You'd better get in the front, Jake," Wally said. "I can drive the old man's tractor."

There was a lot of *ern-a-ern-a erning*, sputtering, stalling and backfiring before the car motor broke into a regular flub and Dan said, "Now, are we all set?"

"Let 'er go," Wally said. There was low angry whine.

"Put in the clutch, Dan," Wally said.

"Yeah, forgot that." Finally the motor gunned and we jerked ahead. "Here we go."

"Hold her, Dan, there's a stop sign!"

The car snubbed short and Wally lurched forward, jamming Dan's nose into the steering wheel.

"Get off me head."

"All clear?"

"All clear."

"Let go of the wheel, Dan… You got to let go of the wheel!"

"Right, Wally, right, right!"

"Dan, you got to leave the wheel alone."

"Hold 'er!" I said. "Wait for that car…*whooof*."

"I can't see," Wally said.

"You don't have to. Go straight. Straighten out some more. There…look out, look out! Left, Wally, left."

"Here we go," Dan said.

By the time we got to the edge of town—after sideswiping a light pole, roaring in and out of a low ditch and knocking a few pickets out of someone's fence—things pretty well levelled off. Then it was a matter of staying in the middle of the road (we took to the back roads), hoping we wouldn't meet another car (we didn't) until we got home.

We didn't quite make it. Dan's gateway was a little small, and the old car's lights, not much better than candles, weren't much help. We tilted over the edge of the culvert and rammed the right front wheel into the far shoulder of the ditch. Wally was thrown over Dan's head into the windshield. I could hear them clawing and scratching in the darkness before the door opened and they half tumbled out just as the motor stalled.

"You okay, Dan?" I said.

"Yup."

"Want a hand in?"

"Nope, I'm just going to sit for a while."

"Goodnight, Dan," I said. "Thanks."

"Welcome as the flowers in May."

I could see Wally's dim form striding away in the weak glow from Dan's yard light as I got out of the car. I caught up.

"The old buzzard," Wally seethed through his teeth. "He could have gotten us killed. I got a bump on me head big as a goose egg."

"Saturday night just ain't what it used to be," I said.

"I ain't going anywhere with that old beggar again," Wally said. And he kept muttering away like a dog gnawing a bone. We were pretty well up to Tom Dougal's gate before he cooled down.

"What's on TV now?" I said.

"The news, then the fat lady sings. Coming in?"

"Might as well; can't dance."

"Ain't too hot at giving directions, either."

"Well, your steering ain't anything to brag about."

Prelude to
The End on Hook Road

Progress in diverse ways and measures, with the anaesthesia of better, easier times, had converged on Hook Road in such a short time that virtually no one could have totally predicted the outcome. In actual fact, the changes introduced, understood to become part of the set farming community life in general, never did. Instead, they became catalysts for change of a broader scope.

The small compact tractor, for all its work-saving and convenience, never completely meshed with horse machinery. In many instances, what one man could handle with horses, now took two: one to tend the implement and the other to drive the tractor. Minds began turning toward tractor-made machinery: side delivery rakes, balers and whatnot—even self-propelled grain and potato combines were standing in the wings. Electricity not only opened the way to modern convenience, but also did away with the old methods of preserving food, leading to reliance on food stores. Easy financing became no more than an enticement toward more borrowing. And it all combined to draw away from the simple, hands-on methods geared to keep down the overhead.

TV, with its worlds of captivating wonder, rapidly became a replacement for the gabfest and the card games; the convenient transportation brought on by the car expanded visitation beyond the local; the new song and dance of rock and roll obliterated the square dance and overshadowed country music for the youth. Those relied on to carry on tradition all hit at community interaction, the very core of community life. Simply, the small farming community had been seduced.

A strange lethargy set in along Hook Road, as if people were waiting on something to come. It wasn't long before that something made itself known. Within a few short years, it became apparent that the small farms could not produce enough to keep up with the bills. It was either get big or get out. Some hung on for a while, renting their land to bigger farmers and getting part-time work when they could. Then, except the few who went for expansion, those young enough drifted away to the big cities, factories, mines and forests scattered across the country. The older ones went and finished off their days in the little town or the city.

The End on Hook Road

CHAPTER 8

Things pretty well came apart for us the following fall. It actually began during grain harvest. The Boss had been struggling the last few years with rheumatism, especially at plowing. He would come in from the fields gimping, with his face in a cringe. He used to rub himself a lot with liniment, sometimes soaking his underwear with the stuff—you could smell him coming. But old age was catching up to him, too.

The crunch began on a Saturday evening when we were stooking grain. Rain was on the way and we would have to work late into the night to beat it. The Old Man's walk was slow and hesitant as we made our way back to the field after milking.

"I hate to keep a young fellow working on Saturday night," he said. His voice, cutting out of a gloomy silence, had a subdued, apologetic tone, with just a hint of defeat.

"It's okay," I said. "I don't mind stooking, and it's only

one night."

The darkness came on fast. Before long it was pitch black and we pretty well had to go by feel and foreknowledge.

Amidst the rustle of the sheaves, The Old Man's voice broke in again, tired and gloomy. "You sure you wouldn't sooner go to town? I hate to keep a young fellow from his Saturday night."

"It's okay; too late to go now, anyway," I said.

Then I heard the rustles from his direction become hesitant. Then they stopped.

"I'm going to have to call a day," The Old Man said.

I stopped, and in the silence, disturbed only by cricket creaks, I knew The Old Man was no longer the man he was and he knew it, too.

"I can finish it," I said. "I don't mind stooking."

He hesitated a moment, then I could hear the brush of his footfalls fade into the darkness.

Before the harvest was in, it wasn't hard to tell King and Queen weren't in much better shape than The Old Man was. They, too, had grown slow and stiff and old. Like The Old Man, they did well to get the grain and potatoes in. Bill was sound enough for a few more years, but the others would have to be replaced. One of our relatives on Nanny's side was interested in buying Queen as a pet, but proud and faithful old King would have to go for fox meat.

The day the buyers took him away in a box in the back of a half-ton truck was a sad one. But I'd have to say one of the saddest things I ever saw was him ambling back down the lane the next day, bedraggled and forlorn. He was being held in a corral by the railroad with other fox horses awaiting transport to the factory when they'd broken loose, and he, like so many other times, had made his way back home.

Nanny was in the yard feeding the chickens. The old horse came to her and nuzzled her arm with his muzzle. The Boss was in the shop building a box trap to catch a skunk that had been marauding our hen house. Nanny called to him. He came out with a few sticks of scrap lumber in his hands. He stopped short, staring at King. The sticks fell from his hands. His face went pale. Then a slow, vicious anger crept in. He took King to the watering trough and watered him. Then took him to his stall and fed him. By the time he came back out, the anger on his face had become almost violent. "Go over to Joe's, Jake, and call them fellows up," he said. "Tell them to get out here."

When Mabel relayed the message, I could hear the voice at the other end of the line. Along with being weak, it had a thin whine. When the two fat men got out of their truck that evening, they had that edgy look, like they were approaching something that kicks. They were almost right. I hadn't known that The Boss could hand out such a tongue-lashing. He was almost on tiptoe, sometimes seething through his teeth.

The two men stood like dogs in a hailstorm, and it was "Yes, sir, Mr. Jackson. No, sir, Mr. Jackson."

When The Boss finally ran down and went and got King, the grey-black clouds that had been holding off all day, as if waiting for this precise moment, began to rain.

The Old Man passed the horse back to the buyers, then stood gripping the lead rope. With hunched shoulders and heavy raindrops streaking down on his head, the large drops splattering on his cap peak and knobby hands, he stood watching the truck leave. King's head bobbed and turned, his eye whites flashing, sometimes at The Old Man, sometimes at Bill, who was running and neighing along the pasture fence by the lane.

I don't know if that was when The Boss decided to get the tractor or not. Quite likely he'd decided before, since it was time to start plowing and he had not made any move that I knew of to buy horses. Whatever, the tractor came with a plow the following Saturday—a cool, clear day with a crisp freshness that tuned in with the coloured leaves wisping here and there in the barnyard. The delivery men rolled them, hooked up, off a flatbed truck, handed The Boss a couple of manuals and left without saying much of anything.

The Boss had never driven a motor vehicle of any kind. I hadn't either. He must have spent an hour or more checking things out, flipping through the manuals, pausing at times to peer over the rims of his glasses to check out some object, either on the plow or the tractor. Eventually, he threw a sheepish glance at me, hesitated, took a deep breath, climbed onto the tractor seat, took another look at a manual and sat rigid for a while with both hands on the wheel. Then he flipped out the ignition button and hauled on a rod on the left side of the battery box. Nothing happened. He flipped hastily through the manual again, his eyes shooting alternating glances between the pages and the controls at the battery box. Then he pulled the rod on the right side of the battery box and the starter suddenly gave a cranky, draggy *rhutt* or two and the tractor jerked ahead in jumps until The Boss threw up his hands like he was dropping a hot potato. He paused then and stared at the rod with his head canted. Then he pushed in the clutch with his foot and pulled the rod again and the motor stirred to life, and there was this low, growling whine until he finally released the rod. Then he let the clutch out and the tractor bucked ahead and stalled.

In time, after a lot of gear grinding, jerking, stalling, hitting reverse and jack-knifing into the plow, he got moving, with him sitting straight-armed, straight-backed and heading for the barnyard fence. Before he crashed into the fence, he belched out a shocked "whoa" with his hands flapping and clawing, not knowing what to do. He got stopped without too much damage, except a few paint scratches. Then he was jack-knifed in with the plow and, after some jerking and wheel-twisting, we wound up unhitching to get things straightened out.

He headed out the lane to the field, swerving with wheel jerks, doing his best not crash into a post, and finally got the plowing started, in a kind of way. He'd forget about the wheel now and then or hit the brake instead of the clutch, and he pulled into the headland a few times without tripping out the plow—the furrows were something else—but by noon he had it pretty well down. In the afternoon he went to work to teach me. By mid-afternoon, he left me at it and went and cleaned out the pigs.

But The Old Man didn't seem completely settled on things, even after the plowing was done. It was as if his mind had not been completely made up concerning what direction he was taking. Then the double whammy came and helped make up his mind for him.

The Boss usually left the stock out as long as there was a hint of pasture. It usually took a cold rain or a wet snow to prod him into bringing them all in for the winter. It was a wet snow that fall that did it, and the animals were cold-soaked, with that dirty wet-hair smell, and the barnyard was a sticky goo.

The milk cows weren't a problem. We were able to herd the spring calves into a big pen by the barn floor without too much trouble. The fun started when we began putting the young cattle into stalls, with them half wild and nervous, having not seen the inside of the barn since spring. You had to be ready to dodge a careless horn. They could bolt in an instant, and some had to be roped and tail-twisted in. We were working a big steer along the fence leading to the horse stable, with The Boss on the rope and me twisting his tail on the fence side. Suddenly, the steer snapped his rear end and whammed me against the fence, then bolted, knocking The Boss down. The Boss had the rope wound around his arm and couldn't get free. By the time I got hold of things, the steer had dragged him pretty much the length of the barnyard through the muck and manure. It was tricky business getting The Boss free of the rope with my feet slewing in the muck and the steer twitching and bolting. When I finally did, The Old Man staggered to his feet, and, after few starts, wobbled to the fence and leaned on a post.

"I'll look after the rest," I said. "You'd better go into the house."

He didn't answer, just stood catching his breath. Eventually, he staggered in a hunch to the house.

At supper, The Boss sat unusually quiet, picking at his food.

I did the barn work myself. When I came in, he was sitting smoking his pipe with that same quietness. The evening news was just beginning. Nanny was trimming the lamp wick with a pair of scissors. When she lit the lamp, the weak glow didn't change much except to shadow the walls and throw a glint into the cap peak shadow on The Old Man's face.

Except for his lips, curling around his pipe now and then, letting out puffs of smoke, his face was completely deadpan. I took off my boots and coat and sat with my feet on the oven door and let the warmth of the stove pull away the dampness and chill. I pulled out my makings and rolled a smoke. I had been smoking since spring then, and it was still enjoyment, not the puff and choke habit it turned out to be. Nanny moved a chair over beside me and went at her knitting. We listened to the news and weather until it finished and the evening mass came on and Nanny went and turned off the radio and came back and sat working out a missed stitch. We sat saying nothing for a spell, enjoying the warmth of the kitchen.

Eventually, The Old Man took out his pipe and began taking sidelong glances at me. When he finally spoke, his voice was quiet, blunt and resolved. "What do you plan to do with your life?" he said. He sat peering at me, waiting for an answer.

I had been pondering the future since one evening the previous summer when I was walking in our lane from shooting crows, with my twenty-two rifle under my arm. It was one of those quiet gloomy evenings just before a squall. Somehow, the peacefulness of the grazing cattle in the pasture field by the lane, the lonely chirps of birds in the woods and the softness of the breeze seemed to combine with the mood of the evening to say in unison that I didn't belong here anymore and that I would soon have to leave. But I had no definite direction, none in the least, actually.

"I don't know," I said.

The Old Man took a deep breath and let it out.

"Well, I'm going to work at shutting her down," he said. "Me and Ella have been talking about it. I'll get someone to help us thrash the grain all at once; move the potatoes out, they're not a bad price now; Fred James will take them out and grade them." He paused and looked at the floor. "I'm not half man anymore; that's all there is to it. I plan to keep some beef and a few milk cows, grow grain and hay, get someone to custom combine the grain, custom bale the hay. There'll be no more potatoes. In two years' time I'll be pensioned off. I'll either rent or sell." The Old Man's voice was quiet and steady and completely determined. His mind was made up. He was used to making hard decisions and living with the outcome and there was no sign of flinching. "I was planning for Waldron to take over, but…" His voice trailed off. He straightened and paused, looking full at me. "You're a good little worker, but you're no farmer. It's not in you. I was hoping you'd get an education. It's not too late; we could help you there." The Old Man paused again, his eyes searching my face. I made no reply. "Whatever," The Old Man said firmly. "You're old enough to start out on your own. You're welcome to make this place a place to come to as long as we're around, but between now and next spring you need to be thinking about finding work and making your own way."

"We're not telling you to leave right away," Nanny said. "You can work out and be here until you get used to things. Maybe shovel snow this winter for the railroad. Agnes told me Fred James was looking for a worker for the warehouse."

It all kind of grabbed me pretty hard. I had been sailing along, waiting for things to take their course, with the security of a set home life. Suddenly, that security was being swept away from me and for the first time I had to face life on my own.

"You're a young man now," The Old Man said. "The whole world lays before you, but the time will sneak by. You can't waste it. The younger you learn that the better." The Old Man packed his pipe again and lit up and thought for a while before he spoke again. There was just the sound of Nanny's knitting needles above the crack and burr of the stove. "And you got to be looking down the road. You'll be married some-day, with children. You need to be thinking about that responsibility and it's a big one. You need to be thinking about being a provider and that means you got to be prepared to have regular work. If you don't want to get a full education, at least get a trade. Go to work for a carpenter or a plumper, learn the trade. You try carpentry and you don't like it, stay at it until you get it down anyway. All work is related. You get to be a good carpenter you'll know things that will help you if you try something else and you'll have that to fall back on." The Old Man paused again and studied the floor. Then he sighed, belched out smoke and eyed me sidewise again. "Anything you learn in life will be of use to you one way or another. And try anything; don't be afraid to fail. There's no shame in failing; the shame is in not trying." The Old Man sighed again and leaned back in his chair. "The rest is up to you, I guess."

We talked about the subject again a few times before winter. By then, the grain was threshed, the potatoes were sold and moved out and the wood was sawed. After the first big storm I hired on with Fred James. I boarded at home half the winter, then went for room and board at Mrs. Deighan's. She was a widow in the village.

That's pretty well how I left Hook Road. Not much more to it. I went back to visit, of course. But the road was never the same after. Once you leave a place, you see it from a different perspective, and the place wasn't the same, anyway; the old communal spirit was gone, among other things. The changes on Hook Road snowballed after I left. Add a few short years and it was pretty much as it is now.

The Old Man was the first to go. He put in a crop of grain and did pretty well what he said, but his old frame couldn't handle things even with what he had. The following spring he held a sale. Most everyone on the road showed up, though most of them didn't buy that much. The old farm fraternity, what was left of it, had something to do with bringing them out; but I'd have to say mostly it was because the reality of the beginning of the end of Hook Road community was hitting home. You could see that in the sombreness everyone affected through the whole sale. The auctioneer, a skinny, sharp-faced, jovial type, who had a joke with every article, soon gave up his quips after getting nothing but deadpan expressions from the crowd.

Nanny busied herself as usual, always her way of dealing with whatever. She helped organize the sale trail. The Old Man sat in the old armchair in the yard, whittling at a stick, pausing at times to glance up at something being sold. There was a firm tightness to his mouth and his eyes would grow misty and he'd look down to hide it. When they auctioned Bill off, he couldn't take it anymore—went and hid in the horse stable. When he came back they were into the household articles and the armchair was gone.

One by one, with the curt spasmodic bid shouts from the crowd spacing into the auctioneer's singsong, ending with the stark finality of his "sold," the articles worth next to nothing in their usefulness, priceless in their memories and meaning, disappeared into a sea of indifference. And as they went, those that did (most of the horse machinery didn't), the sombreness grew. It was sad to see it all go, like watching something die. As they were selling the property, I noticed the old light wagon standing battered and all but paintless by itself in the barnyard. I could have cried.

The farm went to Angus Simms. He was expanding on his back property south of Jar Road, just across from ours. The Old Man and Nanny lived out their days in a little house they bought in town.

Joe Mason packed it in a few years later; sold out to Tom Dougal. His back went bad and he was over his head in debt anyway. He had a brother in Toronto; moved up there, got a job as a janitor in a big school. Wally wound up there, too. Joe got a toupée about the time Wally's head was beginning to smooth off and he got the idea to start a wig shop. Last I heard, he was still at it. Linda Robins just *happened* to wind up there, too. She finally nailed Wally down. They wound up with a house full of kids.

Alban Gallant sold out to James not long after Joe left; moved into the city and ran the new rink they built there until he retired, His daughter, Candide, was the county beauty queen one year.

John Cobly took cancer not six months after Alban left; died within a month. James got his farm, too. Agnes went to live with one of their daughters.

Jim Mackie was next to go, though not by much. He moved to Sault Saint Marie, Ontario; got work handling a crane. I heard he won a fiddle contest up there. Tom Dougal got his farm, too.

Dan Coulter took a bit of a twist. He got watching some TV evangelist and caught religion; quit the booze and whatnot. He sold out to Hallis Main, who joined his own property to Dan's on the west side about the time Jim left. Dan moved into town; got to be quite the churchgoer—even did a little lay preaching. The church he went to pretty much buried him when he went out. He had no children and no living relatives.

Things went bad all the way around for the Wallaces. Charlie's marriage went sour before too long. Joanie didn't seem to fit into the Wallace scene too well, and Charlie got into the booze a bit heavy over things. The marriage blew to pieces and Joanie took off with an airman. Charlie moved into the city and went to work with Alban Gallant at the rink and played hockey with the senior team there, when he was sober. The liquor got him pretty bad. He was a hockey bum for a while, played Allan Cup–calibre in Ontario until the booze took him down. Last I heard, he was a skid row bum in Toronto and Wally and Joe Mason were trying to bring him around.

Alf went kind of soft in the head at the last. I was down fishing at the creek one Labour Day and caught him sitting hunched over on a block in the shop with his arms dangling off his knees. The ashes in the forage were crusted and grey like they'd been there for a long time. Off to the side, the wood sleigh he had started about five years before sat with an auger sticking up from a half-finished hole in one of the bunks and there was a cobweb running from a handle tip to the middle of the bunk.

He didn't reply right away when I spoke; just sat looking at me with his eyes slightly staring and his face slack. When he finally did, it was in a low monotone, melancholy and distant: "Used to make knives from files, skates, too," he said. "Fixed the lock on Harvey's musket back then. Shod twelve horses in one day and I was an inventor and…" Then George came in.

"Come on, Alf," he said. "I need you to help me get that fence fixed. No good in you sitting here all day, mooning."

"I'll be right with you," Alf said.

"No, you won't," George said. "No, you won't. You'll sit here all day, mooning. Now come on, with Charlie gone you're going to have to pitch in. There's no more horses to shoe and your inventing never got you anywhere and never will."

I decided to leave. Alf wound up in a mental institution. George carried on for a while with Hilda working in the food plant, the big concern built just outside of town. Then he rented to James and went to work in the plant, too. He finally sold out to James and moved to town.

Tom Dougal hung on the longest; went into dairy. Then he decided to go bigger and by then there wasn't any more available property nearby so he sold out to Simms and moved out west.

There were only the big tractors and big machines of the modern era riding on the road then, when they needed to, and the odd vehicle taking a shortcut. Gradually, the houses and farm buildings—with windows like sad, vacant eyes—became dilapidated, their roofs back-sprung, their sides bulging.

One by one, they were burned and their cellars were filled in, until they were all gone, completing the obliteration of what was once the Hook Road.

EPILOGUE

It has been reported, or imagined, or whatever, that ghosts of the past hang around places that have been vacated. I don't experience any such phenomena on Hook Road anytime I'm around. Too bad there isn't such a thing; might enhance whatever memories and nostalgia I might be able to scare up. The various outside connections that played their part in Hook Road life don't help much, either. One of the problems is that whatever brings familiarity is pretty much overcome by what's changed, new or missing in its surroundings.

In the village the railroad winds through like a grassy path, stripped naked by the absence of ties and rails and the station and warehouses that ran beside it. Standing by it, it's hard to imagine a steam engine idling with its chant, its steam and coal smoke sweeping over warehouse men loading a box car, banking a wagon rig and its driver pulling away from the general store, sweeping upward and fading into nothing.

A car door slams from farther up. A resident getting set to

commute to work or some other function. He merely lives here, knows nothing of the local past and probably wouldn't be interested anyway.

There are other survivors: the church and the hall, but they're surrounded by big modern houses and don't fit anymore; the school, but it's been renovated into a house and made a misfit more than the others. It's hardly worth mentioning the few old houses in a row, two of them in broken-down gloom with their roofs caved in, their yard fences with pickets pointing in crazy directions, broken and matted with weeds. The silence of the place has an eeriness to those who knew what it was. There's more life in the graveyard now; at least you can experience the familiarity of the names.

In the town, there's action at Tim Horton's, the quick-pick store, the pharmacy and the craft shop. You can get liquor at a vendor's. If you're a tourist, you can have a look at the railroad artifacts and pictures at the rebuilt station house or rent a bicycle for a ride on the rail trail. All other venues of importance—the funeral parlour, bank, rink and the rest—are in the outskirts.

It's quite a modern town now, with new buildings differently arrayed than the old so that you'd have trouble reckoning where the horse shed and a lot of other places were. The buildings remaining have been made to fit in, like the grocery store, whose rustic appearance coincides with the craft shop's.

The town is modern, clean and functional and you can stand at a corner on a Saturday night and catch absolutely nothing of the buzz and festive excitement of an evening once so special or what made it that in a time so different from long ago. So wide is the gulf.

But time and change go hand in hand. And change will come whatever and there's no going back. The changes to Hook Road came swift, diverse and so complete that, when you look things over, all that really remains lives in the hearts and minds of those of us who lived there, and we grow increasingly few.

But to this writer's experience and knowledge, there have been few if any progress-related change sweeps that were so sudden and complete as the changes that happened on Hook Road. But it's interesting to note that, in a fleeting moment, usually at the funeral of another missing link, where we comment on how it takes a funeral to bring us together, hands clasp and eye contact is made and a thousand things lived to the point of needing no mention flood in and we're just as much a part of Hook Road as we ever were.

Home Again

How would it be, I wonder, to walk once more through the fields, with their gentle roll, while a friendly moon spreads its bask on the crusted snows of March and fence posts, showing white on their snow side, stand in line like old friends.

I went home to visit on such a night, from the village where I stayed when I worked for the potato farmer.

I can remember finding the latch on the solid old front door by knowing where it should be in the darkened porch, still smelling of potatoes and clay.

The kitchen somehow seemed smaller as I stepped inside, but the old oil lamp on the table gave the same shallow, friendly glow it used to. We sat around the cheery old stove with our feet on the oven door in sort of a huddle, just like we used to, especially during the fierce storms that used to snuff cold and snow through the cracks. There were jokes, twenty questions, talk of almost a year's happenings and lunch.

And then I walked back to the village, my future bobbing like the dark shadows before me.

The years have gone somehow and the future fades into the past. The chances of life have wrought their change. Yet I wonder, how it would be, on an evening by the light of a bright March moon, my feet crunching on crusted snow, to visit home once more.